Praise for Ghosters . .

"A creaky old house, ghost sightings, and the forbidden third floor will engage young readers all the way through to the unexpected ending. An exciting debut novel full of mystery and humor. Diana Corbitt is a terrific writer. "
—Carrie Bedford, author of the Kate Benedict paranormal mystery series

"Be prepared for a wild ride as Theresa, Kerry and Joey explore their new home, a rundown Victorian mansion. Get ready for what they find when they get up the nerve to go into the basement. And hang onto your seat when they venture upstairs and through the door Theresa's Dad forbade her to go through. Ghosters is great fun. It is well paced with wonderful quirky characters that readers will love."—J.P. Shaw, author of *Drazil House*

GHOSTERS 2

REVENGE OF THE LIBRARY GHOST

GHOSTERS 2

REVENGE OF THE LIBRARY GHOST

DIANA CORBITT

A Dragonfeather Book
Bedazzled Ink Publishing Company * Fairfield, California

978-1-945805-85-1 paperback

Cover Design
by

DESiGNS

Dragonfeather Books
a division of
Bedazzled Ink Publishing Company
Fairfield, California
http://www.bedazzledink.com

*My thanks to my family, all my writing buddies,
and my favorite librarian.*

CHAPTER 1

"THIS IS CRAZY," my big sister Theresa says. "Never ever *ever* would I even think about spending the night in that place."

I focus on keeping my bike steady as I turn my head to ask, "Why shouldn't I sleep at Elbie's? Don't you like him?"

"Liking Elbie has nothing to do with it."

Since Dad won't be home until eight, Theresa and her English friend, Kerry, are helping me bring my overnight stuff to Elbie's house. Like a lot of people with Asperger's Syndrome, I'm not super coordinated, and I think they're worried I'll crash my bike into a tree if I try to lug everything there myself.

For a while, we pedal on in silence as I try to figure out what Theresa meant. Still confused, I ask the same question of Kerry. Like Theresa, Kerry's in eighth grade, and at six-foot-two, looks a little strange clutching my Spiderman sleeping bag as she pedals down the street.

"Elbie's pleasant enough," Kerry answers. "When he's not being silly."

True enough. Elbie's a good friend, but his obsession with pranking people can get annoying. "Well, Dad likes Elbie's dad," I say, returning my concentration to the street ahead of us. "He likes their house too."

With my bed pillow tucked under her left arm like a football, Theresa looks back at me as we turn the next corner. "Yeah, I've seen it," she tells me. "It's an awesome house. And I'm sure the whole family is great. It's just that—"

"Is it because they're black?"

"What? No—I mean . . ." The school Elbie and I go to is coming up on the right.

Theresa waves us into the Fern Creek Elementary parking lot, now empty because it's Saturday.

"The fact that the Birds are black has nothing to do with it," she says as she and Kerry pull to a stop in the wide-open bus area. "For crabs sakes, Jojo, they live in a funeral home."

My brakes squeak as I pull to a stop in front of her. "Not *in* a funeral home. *Over* a funeral home. And it's not the way you think. The living area is on the top floor. All the mortuary stuff is downstairs, the flowers . . . the caskets . . ."

"The dead bodies?" Kerry says.

"Of course, the dead bodies. Why would they bring them upstairs?"

Since all the girls do is raise their eyebrows, I adjust the straps of my backpack and continue my defense. "No, the bodies definitely stay in the basement—except for when Elbie's dad brings them up to the chapel. That's on the main floor. You know, in a way, Dad and Mr. Bird are a lot alike. They're both around forty . . . they both work at home . . ."

"All that may be true," Kerry says. "But your father writes books. He doesn't—"

"Whoa-whoa-whoa." Theresa waves both hands in Kerry's face. "Please, don't go there."

AFTER PROMISING THERESA to never discuss the details of Elbie's family business in front of her, we continue on our way, and, five minutes later, come to a stop in front of Elbie's house. Aside from the white picket fence surrounding the front yard, the funeral home isn't much different than our place. Like our own Victorian, there's a wide wooden porch, lots of detailing, and tons of windows, many of which are bordered with stained glass.

Since Elbie's got ADHD, I'm not surprised to spot him practicing his skateboard tricks a few houses down. I call him over, and he shows off a flip trick as he zooms down the sidewalk toward us. Once everyone says hi, I climb off my bike and Kerry passes him my sleeping bag.

The biggest difference between Elbie's house and mine is the black and white *VIRTUE FUNERAL HOME* sign sticking out of the lawn behind the white waist-high fence.

Theresa studies it as she climbs off her bike. "Established in 1954? That's a lot of funerals."

"Got that right," Elbie says. "My Great-grandpa Bird bought the place over sixty years ago." He lifts his chin. "Counting me, that'll be four generations of Bird morticians."

"Interesting," Theresa says. "I wouldn't think you'd be into that stuff."

"But why did your great-grandfather name it Virtue Funeral Home?" Kerry says. "Why not Bird Funeral Home?"

"Oh, he did," Elbie tells us, "but that just confused people. For the first two weeks, the only business he got was a guy with two mallard ducks and an old lady with a dead parrot in her purse."

The girls trade looks. Never good at reading facial expressions, I ignore it and allow Theresa to give me a quick goodbye hug. She hands me my pillow, and Elbie holds the gate open so I can roll my bike through.

"We'll chain it up with mine later," Elbie tells me.

I park my bike and follow him up to the front entrance where a huge fluffy cat waits by the front door.

Elbie grins as it sniffs my shoes. "Aaaaw, Skunky misses you. Go on. Pet him."

Black with a white stripe down his back, the little monster is perfectly named. "No thanks," I say, keeping my distance. "I'm not getting my arms clawed again."

Elbie chuckles as he tugs open the front door. A sofa and several armchairs decorate the lobby along with three tall plants of different species. As usual, there's a vase of flowers on the round table in the middle of the room. Sometimes it's filled with roses from Mrs. Bird's garden, but today, it's a mixture of flowers I can't name. Elbie walks past the table and stops, surprised by the crowd milling around inside the chapel.

"Who are all those people?" I ask him.

Elbie smacks his head like a kid who just realized it was Picture Day. "Doggone it. I forgot the five o'clock service. Upstairs," he whispers. "Fast."

In order to reach the big staircase, we have to walk right past the open chapel doors and a little sign announcing the five o'clock service is for someone named Nelly Dysert. Even though I'm not particularly fond of looking at dead people, my eyes are drawn to the large glass panels separating the chapel from the lobby. The far wall of the chapel is all but covered with flowers, with a pale pink casket resting right in the middle, the top part open wide. Inside, lies Nelly Dysert. A nice-looking old black lady, from what I can see of her profile.

Elbie's dad is standing beside the casket, speaking to some people, and they stop talking as I wave hi. No one waves back, and we reach the stairs as Mr. Bird shuts the chapel doors.

"Uuuuugh," Elbie says, sighing loudly. "I just remembered I was supposed to bring you in the back way."

"Are you in trouble?"

"Naw. My folks are used to me forgetting things."

With an "oh well" shrug, he dropkicks my sleeping bag up the big wooden staircase and jogs after it. I follow, pillow slung over one shoulder like a bag of Santa's toys.

"It always smells good in here." I draw in another deep breath. "Obviously, it's because of the flowers but there's a lemony scent too."

"Dawg, that's just my Mom's furniture polish. I don't smell it or the flowers anymore. Guess when you live your whole life around certain smells, your nose gets used to them."

"More like your brain. When an odor is continuous, the brain decides to ignore it in order to put its processing powers to better use. It's called habituation."

Elbie looks at me sideways. "Okay, brainiac. Where'd you learn all that?"

"My dad is always telling me not to focus my interest on bugs so much, so I watched a TV special on the five senses. I figure since my Asperger's makes me sensitive to certain sensations, I should learn more about it."

"Smart. My dad loves little fun facts like that. You should repeat it to him."

"Okay." I prop my pillow against the bannister and trot back down to the lobby, backpack bouncing.

"Hey, wait." Elbie follows. "Man, I didn't mean right this minute."

"Why not?" I stop outside the chapel doors.

"Because there's a lot of sad people at that service. You can't just blast in there chitchatting about nose smells. It would be . . ."

"Unkind? Callous?"

"If callous means rude, then yeah." He herds me back toward the staircase. "No worries. Saved by the bell, right?"

"I didn't hear any bell."

"Me. I'm the bell."

I look him up and down. "You look nothing like a bell, so I'm guessing that was a metaphor."

"Meta-who?" Elbie grins. As always, his slightly gapped teeth remind me of swollen Tic Tacs against his dark skin. "Come on, dawg. Let's get on up to my room. I wanna see what you brought."

But before our feet touch the first step, a familiar feeling tickles the back of my neck. "There's a ghost nearby."

Elbie nods. "Most spirits like to attend their own services. It's probably Mrs. Dysert."

We look around, but don't see any ghosts yet. Halfway up, we spot the old black woman. I know it's her because she's wearing the same pink dress as her body down in the chapel.

Mrs. Dysert smiles at Elbie. "Hello again. Who's your friend?"

"This is my little brother, Joey."

She glances down at his brown arm, which is right next to my pinkish one.

"Oh, uh," Elbie smiles, "he's adopted."

"Isn't that interesting. Pleased to meet you, Joey."

Why did Elbie say that? I'm not his brother, and certainly not his little brother as I'm three months older and two inches taller. Since I'm used to people saying things that make absolutely no sense to me, I let it go and answer with, "Nice to meet you too, Mrs. Dysert." Theresa says it's good to compliment people, so I add, "I saw your casket down in the chapel. It really matches your dress."

"My casket?" She checks her watch and groans. "For heaven's sake. I'm missing my own funeral." Muttering to herself, Mrs. Dysert clutches the railing and hustles down the steps.

"Ma'am," Elbie calls after her in a loud whisper.

"Yes, dear?"

"Don't forget to put yourself on stealth mode."

Her gray head tips to one side. "Stealth what?"

Elbie holds up his hands, fingers waggling. "Someone might see you, ma'am."

"Oh, my!" She creases her brown forehead. "So many things to remember now. I certainly don't want to give somebody a heart attack." With a waggle of her own fingers, she gives me an embarrassed smile, then vanishes.

"I'm not sure why," Elbie says, "but for some reason dead folks find it really hard to keep track of time."

CHAPTER 2

WITH MRS. DYSERT gone, Elbie's smile turns into a full-blown grin. "You know, besides me, you're the bravest kid in our whole school."

"Why do you say that?" I ask as we start down the hall toward his room.

"All the other kids at school are so scared of seeing a ghost they won't even set one toe in The Home. But ask Joey Martinez to spend the night and all he says is 'What games do I bring?'"

"It's not courage if there's nothing to be afraid of. All those kids know about ghosts is what they see on TV."

"I'm not buying it. We're brave. Probably because of our conditions. Kind of like superheroes."

"I don't know about ADHD, but being unafraid of spirits is not one of the recognized characteristics of my Asperger's."

"Whatever. I'm still not buying it."

Not sure how to respond, I say, "Good, because I'm not selling it." My words must surprise him, because, for once, Elbie doesn't have a smart comeback.

"I like talking to ghosts," I say, realizing it as I speak. "That's probably good since I see them all the time now. At the supermarket, the gas station . . ."

"Yeah, me too. My dad says it's like exercising a muscle. The more ghosts you see, the easier it gets."

"I think he's right. But I'm still confused. Those other ghosts are different from the ones here. They don't look half as . . . as . . ."

"Real?" He tosses my sleeping bag in the corner as we step into his bedroom. The skateboard, he drops in the middle of the floor. "There are good reasons for that. If it's going to manifest, a ghost has to have some kind of power source. Some ghosts are good at finding them. Others aren't. And how long they've been dead has something to do with it too. Mortuary ghosts are brand new. Plus, when you add in the proximity . . ."

As Elbie talks, I breathe in the smell of his room. At first, I thought it was salad dressing, but Elbie says it's olive oil, which he sometimes rubs on his hair to keep it from getting dry. Most people wouldn't notice it, but I'm pretty sensitive to smells.

"What's a proximity?" I say as I pick my way to the bed, careful not to step on all the marbles and Legos which cover the floor like sprinkles on a doughnut.

"It means closeness," Elbie explains. "The first and easiest power source a ghost learns to use is their own body. My dad says the closer a spirit stays to its body, the more lifelike it appears. See, the body is like a big old battery. And, like all batteries, sooner or later the juice runs dry."

"Oh, yeah, juice." Since my sister explained the term to me last month, I know Elbie's talking about electricity and not actual squeezed fruit. "It makes sense. That's why the ones who have been dead a long time have to find some other source to drain their energy from when they want to be seen. Like camera batteries or the heat from the air." I push some action figures off the bed to make a space where I can set down my backpack. "Do you ever confuse ghosts with live people?"

"Only when they're far away. Remember the weird feeling you got just before we saw Mrs. Dysert?"

"Yes."

"Well, there's usually that. But if you're not sure, just look at their feet."

"Why their feet?"

"Because they float." He holds his fingers about a quarter inch apart. "Like this far off the ground."

I nod and head over to the bookcase to look at the new game Elbie got to rent. "Oh, cool, Dino-Slayer 2. I brought my Dino-Slayer 1 game . . . *and* some 3-D insect puzzles."

"Ooooh, insects. What a shocker."

"Why are you surprised? You know how much I like— wait. Was that a joke?"

"Kinda. More like sarcasm." Elbie takes the rented game from my hand and sets it back on the shelf alongside his TV. "My folks want us to leave the video games for later. Let's go out in the backyard."

We bounce on the trampoline for a while, then play HORSE. Elbie must be having a bad day, because unlike at Fern Creek Elementary, where he usually kicks my butt, here he misses most of his shots and soon wants to head inside to try my insect puzzles. But that doesn't go so well either, and after ten minutes of working on the black widow spider, he gives up, claiming it's missing a piece of its right front leg.

"That's impossible," I tell him. "I was really careful to get all the pieces back in the box." I get up to drink some of the strawberry smoothie Mrs. Bird made us and find the missing spider piece lying next to my glass. "See?" I toss it back to him.

He grumbles something I can't understand, then checks the time on his cell phone. "Man, it's already six and my mom hasn't called us down to eat yet. Sure hope Ms. Dysert's service doesn't run too much longer. I am so ready for that pizza." He kicks one of the scattered marbles in my direction. "My nana mailed me a box of those the other day, but they didn't come with instructions. Ever play?"

"I've never even touched one before."

"Well, start touching. You gather them up while I Google marble games."

IT BARELY TAKES Elbie a minute to find a website with instructions for all sorts of marble games. The first one we play is *Boss out*. Then we play *Chasies*. We're just starting a game called *Ring Taw* when Mrs. Bird calls us down to eat. Starving, we drop the marbles and run down to the kitchen where Mr. and Mrs. Bird are already sitting at the table. After a quick prayer, Mrs. Bird starts dishing out pizza slices. Because of Elbie's ADHD diet, the pepperoni pizza is gluten free, but I eat a lot of non-gluten food too, so I'm used to the chewy dough.

Once we're done eating, we head back to play with the Legos I brought, my newest set, the Star Wars Deathstar. After clearing away the marbles, we dump the pieces out in the middle of Elbie's big round area rug. Strangely, the pieces he's looking for always end up by me.

Halfway finished, a frustrated Elbie picks up his cell phone and checks the time. "Finally. It's after eight. Now we can try out that game I rented." His smile drops away. "Man, what is it with this thing lately?"

He holds the phone for me to look at. The little battery icon at the top of the screen is blinking red.

"Four percent!" Elbie growls. "And I haven't even played one game on it today."

Grumbling, he hooks the phone to his charger and pops Dino-Slayer 2 into his game console. At first, Elbie does really well, but around eleven, things change.

"This controller is all jacked up," he tells me after my hunter avatar easily knocks out his t-rex with a giant punch to the belly. "The A button only works half the time." Moments later, his controller stops working altogether. "Great, now the batteries in this thing are dead." He tosses it aside. "Let's play something that doesn't need electricity."

"Okay." I pick up some Legos and the tiny plastic Darth Vader. "Want to finish the Death Star?"

"Naaaah. I need to move." He slouches back on his beanbag chair, then sits up suddenly. "We can play ping pong."

"You have a ping pong table?" I look around the room.

"Not here. Downstairs. In the basement."

"You mean where your dad stores the dead bodies?"

"It would be weird if he kept live ones down there."

Normally, I'd jump at the chance to play ping pong, but my stomach's gone all wormy. It's not that I'm afraid of dead bodies. I'd just rather not be around them. Partly because they make me think of the haunted house in Madame Tussaud's Wax Museum, but mostly because they remind me of my mom's funeral.

Elbie leaps to his feet and pulls me up with him. "Come on. It'll be fun."

CHAPTER 3

SOMETHING MUST SHOW on my face, because Elbie says, "Come on dawg. It's not like we'll have to clear the stiffs off the ping pong table before we can play. There's more than one room down there, remember? Plus, at this hour, all the bodies will already be on ice."

I glance at what's left of my strawberry smoothie. "Ice?"

"That's just what my dad calls it. Come on, I'll show you. Just try not to talk too loud."

We tiptoe downstairs to the now empty lobby. There's a small desk lamp lighting the guestbook pedestal, so the chapel is dim, as well as the hallway leading to the basement door.

"Why don't you turn on some lights?" I ask Elbie as we walk past his dad's office and the meeting room.

"Now why would I do that when the casket room looks so creepy this way?" He tips his head at the open doorway on our right and smiles. In this light, all I can see are rectangular shadows. "Want to try one out?"

"No, and you asked me that the last time we came through here. I don't get your fascination. They're just big fancy boxes."

"Well, if that's true, then how come you never want to climb inside one?"

"Because if I climbed in, you would shut the lid and lock it."

He nods. "True. I guess you know me better than I thought you did."

At the end of the hall is a door marked *PRIVATE.* Elbie opens it wide. "Now I *do* have to turn on the lights. Without them it would be black as my Uncle Chancy down there."

He flicks the switch and we head down the concrete stairs. "You know, one time when I was really little, I got up in the middle of the night whining about needing to use the bathroom. But when my dad stuck me in front of the toilet, I started crying."

"Why?"

"That's the funny part. I was so sleepy that I thought I'd be peeing into one of the caskets. My dad kept saying, 'Go on, Elbie, do it.' But I just couldn't."

"Why? Are caskets really expensive?"

"Heck, yeah. I knew that even when I was four."

With the basement door open, I sniff the air for formaldehyde, a chemical Mr. Bird uses. I was in third grade the first time I smelled it. The school's science specialist was dissecting a dead frog in front of the class. Most kids were grossed out by all the little frog organs, but it was the odor that bothered me.

When the teacher spotted me holding my nose shut, the corner of his mouth twisted upward. "Seriously?" he muttered. "It's just a preservative."

Whatever. All I knew was that it stunk. As Elbie would say, big time.

Relieved I won't have to hold my nose while I'm playing ping pong, I follow Elbie down.

Even though I haven't been here for a few weeks, nothing has changed much. At the bottom is a wide hallway, open on both ends. Like before, several bubble-wrapped caskets are stacked against the cinderblock walls. Most are gold and silver colored, but one is pink, just like Mrs. Dysert's. The embalming room is to the right. That's where I first met Elbie's dad. A short visit, since Mr. Bird was preparing a body for viewing.

I realize that's where Elbie is taking me, and the worms creep back into my stomach. Luckily, he was telling the truth, and the three stainless steel tables in the center of the floor are unoccupied.

I whisper a little thank-you prayer, then ask, "So where's the ping pong table?"

"Patience." Arms spread wide, he does a little turn. "See? I told you the stiffs are all put away."

"Yeah. That reminds me. You said they'd be on ice, and I don't see any of that here."

"That's just an expression. There's no ice, just a big ol' refrigerator with drawers."

I chew my lip as he guides me past a clothes rod filled with empty hangers to the far side of the room. That wall is covered with eight stainless steel doors, each with a slot for its own little nametag.

"What about playing ping pong?" I ask, realizing the drawers might be filled with bodies.

"Oh, we're gonna play. Since my dad's not here, I thought I'd show you around a little." Elbie points at one of the four doors on the bottom row. "Here's where Ms. Dysert was until about three o'clock this afternoon." He steps to the next door. "This is Mrs. Gomez. Nice lady. We're holding her services next Monday." He checks the tags on the top row of doors. "Empty . . . too gross . . . empty." Smiling, he pats the door on the far end. "This one's kind of interesting. They brought him in last night."

I lean over and read the tag. "Malcolm Prendergast."

"Yeah. Cool dude, but kind of squinty-eyed. Reminds me of that old movie actor, Clint Eastwood, just a whole lot shorter. Mr. P used to ride horses for a living. That's why he's being laid to rest wearing this crazy costume. They're called jockey silks. Want to see?" Elbie grips the handle and looks at me, eyebrows raised.

"No, thanks." Even though I don't think Elbie would stuff his cat into the drawer just to set me up for a scare, I haven't seen Skunky for a while, so I'd rather not take any chances.

"But I wouldn't mind meeting his ghost," I offer, noticing what I think is a look of disappointment. "He's close, isn't he?" I tip back my head and call out, "Mr. Prendergast!"

"Hey, knock that off. You'll wake up my parents."

Ooops. I forgot Mrs. Bird told me they go to bed at eleven.

Elbie motions for me to follow, and we head back the way we came and into the storage room. That's where the ping pong table is, surrounded by all kinds of business and family stuff. Like the basement at my house, there's even an old workbench and above it a whole wall lined with hand tools.

"Ghosts aren't like regular people. Once they're dead, they pretty much do as they please." Elbie clears his throat. "Don't worry. You'll see Mr. Prendergast eventually."

Instead of dead bodies lying on the ping pong table as Elbie joked earlier, Mr. Bird's golf bag is the only thing that has to be cleared away before we can play. Between the two of us, we pick it up and lean it against a stack of bright red suitcases, next to which is a round black barbeque and a shelving rack filled with dusty cardboard containers the size and shape of oversized cereal boxes.

"What are those?" I ask.

"Cremains."

I must look confused because he says, "Peoples' ashes. Most have been here for years, but one's new. Only been here a month."

"But why are they here at all?"

"I guess their relatives didn't want them." When I frown, Elbie lifts his shoulders in what I'm guessing is a what-can-I do shrug. "It happens," he tells me, then picks up a ball and two ping pong paddles from the table. He passes me the red paddle as well as the ball. "Go ahead, serve it to me."

Elbie doesn't know it, but I've played ping pong before. A lot. I let loose a screaming hard serve that barely scrapes the corner. Mouth open like a trout, Elbie stumbles back and catches the ball with his hand.

"Where'd you learn to play, in China?"

"I've never been to China. We had a table back at our old house. Before . . ."

"Oh." He bounces the ball back across the table. "Before your mom died and your family had to move to your grandparents' old house."

"Yeah. It seems like a hundred years ago."

"Well, a lot of good things have happened since then. You guys won that *Ghosters* contest, plus, you met me." He grins across the table at me. "Come on, serve it again. I'm good at this game too, so when I whoop you, try not to wake up my folks with all your crying."

I yawn. Having heard Elbie's trash talk before, I ignore it and slam another hard shot. This time he returns it, and we knock the ball back and forth nearly a dozen times before his hit misses the edge of the table by a hair.

"That's another point for me," I tell him. "Let's just play to ten. I'm getting sleepy."

Elbie agrees, and I serve again. This goes on for several minutes, and through the whole game, the difference in our scores is never more than one point.

"Okay," Elbie says loudly. "The score's tied, nine to nine. We're playing to ten points, so if, for any reason, you aren't able to return my next serve, I win."

"Yes, Elbie, I realize that." I set my feet and as I wait for him to serve, the hairs on the back of my neck stand up. "Hey, I think there's a ghost close by."

"Duh, we're in a mortuary. Now, can we finish this?"

I nod, and just as Elbie serves the ball, a strange looking spirit appears beside me. It's a little old man. Smelling a lot like horses, he's dressed in purple and green jockey silks, and his lips all but touch my ear as he barks, "Miss it!" in a voice that sounds like it's been dragged through gravel.

Startled, I let the ball bounce past me, and Elbie gives a snort so loud I'm amazed a wad of snot doesn't fly out with it.

"I won! I beat you."

As Elbie moonwalks around the table, I glance back and forth between my cheating friend and the smirking ghost, who, as Elbie told me, really does look a lot like Clint Eastwood.

"Okay, kid." Mr. Prendergast turns to Elbie. "I did what you asked. Now make sure *I* get what *I* want."

"You got it, Mr. P."

With a tip of his shiny purple cap, the ghost fades into a mist which swirls up into the air conditioning duct.

"He sure does like fancy exits. I guess it makes sense for a guy who wants to spend eternity dressed in purple and green silk." Elbie turns to me, eyebrows raised. "You aren't mad, are you?"

"It was a pretty good trick." I hold up my hand to bump knuckles, and he jogs over. But instead of bumping, I pull him into a headlock.

"Arrghh!" Elbie growls between clenched teeth. "I thought you said it was a good trick."

"That's right, and so is this."

As Elbie thrashes around trying to free himself, the sound of heavy footsteps clumping down the stairs makes me let go. Dressed in loose-fitting black gym shorts and an old Pittsburg Steelers tee-shirt, Mr. Bird lumbers into the room. Like always, he smells like eucalyptus. Elbie says it's because Mr. Bird rubs something on his head. That's probably true, because it shines like a giant malted milk ball under the bright fluorescent lighting.

"Elbie, stop that shouting," Mr. Bird demands. "What's he done now, Joey?"

I straighten my shirt. "Sorry for waking you, Mr. Bird, but Elbie's a cheater. He got the ghost with the weird costume to make me lose the ping pong game."

"You must be talking about Mr. Prendergast." Mr. Bird turns to Elbie, his thick arms crossed. "Son, what did you promise that old man?"

"Nothing we can't handle, Dad."

"It better not be." Mr. Bird turns to me and smiles. "Sounds like you can see ghosts just as well as Elbie can. That's rare."

"It is? But everyone could see the ghosts on those videos we made."

"I'm talking about seeing spirits naturally, with no technology. I can too, but for me, they're just shadows."

I spot the ping pong ball next to a fifty-gallon barrel of formaldehyde and pick it up. "I didn't realize we were so unique. My sister Theresa can see ghosts too."

"Guess it's inherited." Mr. Bird takes away our paddles and waves us toward the stairs ahead of him. "Now, you boys get on up there. It's time to hit the sack."

I peer back over my shoulder. "Is the sack, upstairs? Why does it need hitting?"

CHAPTER 4

ON MONDAYS, OUR class goes to the library at two-fifteen. As usual, I head straight for the bug books. Elbie's not interested in reading about bugs. These days, he checks out books on machines and architecture, especially the ones with pictures of really old buildings. Since insects and arachnids are right across the aisle from where his books are kept, Elbie follows me to the back of the room.

I'm looking for a new book called *The Ultimate Bugopedia.* I noticed it on display last week, but since I had already checked out two others, wasn't able to get it then. I locate *Bugopedia* on its shelf, but before I can get my hands on it, somebody switches off the lights. It's the middle of the day, but I'm not surprised the place is all but black. The only windows are blocked by dark curtains.

As if my classmates have switches of their own, they all start screaming. Boys. Girls. Everybody except Elbie and me. A big hater of loud noises, I clamp my hands over my ears. Maybe I look goofy, but those high-pitched screams really get to me, and in fifth grade, it's not just the girls who are making them.

Elbie, on the other hand, doesn't seem to mind the commotion. In fact, he lives for this kind of disorganization. It's perfect for what he calls his signature move, *The Creep and Freak.*

Expecting more shouting, I keep my ears covered and follow him into the darkness. His first target seems to be Angela Bloom and Sasha Jefferson, probably the only unrelated black and white twins in existence. They're over by the check-out desk, arms linked together. I know it's them because their identical white skirts stand out in the darkness.

Although Elbie's dark blue sweatshirt doesn't make him totally invisible, it certainly helps, and like a skinny little ninja, he hunches toward the girls, hidden from view by a low bookcase. Even with that, a successful *Creep and Freak* won't be easy. Arms locked, the girls are rotating like the beam on a lighthouse.

One hand down and ready to sprint, Elbie waits until their backs are turned just right, then leaps out to tickle both girls simultaneously. Screeching in stereo, Angela and Sasha whirl around. A four-fisted octopus, their thrashing arms whip through the air. But Elbie's too fast, and there's no target left to hit.

Fascinated, I continue to trail him. He startles one boy by jumping out in front of him, hands raised like claws and roaring like a t-rex. Others he tickles or grabs the back of their necks. Like my sister, who's always edgy when the lights go off, the dark seems to affect these kids, and they all scream. Loud.

Finally, the librarian realizes that if she opens the door she'll let in more light. She announces this, and as she heads off to do so, Elbie goes back to the non-fiction section, probably expecting me to still be there. But I'm not. In fact, I'm right behind him.

Even though I watched Elbie scare half the class, I still don't get why it's so enjoyable. Eager to understand, I grab his shoulders and shout, "Boo!"

Eyes like golf balls, he totters backward, slamming into a low bookcase and toppling the hardbacks standing on display. "Geez, Louise! Dawg, what'd you do that for?"

Before I can answer, the lights turn on, then off again.

"Who keeps doing that?" Ms. Crystal Skyeblu shouts. She's the librarian, who, on the first day of school, proudly declared herself as a second-generation flower child. From the sound of her voice, Ms. Skyeblu is on the opposite side of the room.

"Not me," Elbie calls back. "And Joey is my witness."

For some reason, the kids all giggle at that, but the laughter quickly stops when the lights snap back on, then off, then on again.

"This is getting old," Angela Bloom says.

"Very old," Sasha Jefferson says.

Eyes narrowed into slits, they glare at Elbie as they smooth each other's hair and matching pink blouses. My teacher's been showing me how to read facial expressions, I try to read theirs.

"I don't think they liked being scared," I tell Elbie who shrugs and gives them his best *Who, me?* look.

A deep rumbling sound comes from Ms. Skyeblu's throat as she rushes past us, her long carroty hair and patchwork hippy skirt flowing out behind her. The scent she's trailing reminds me of our basement last winter.

"Okay, everybody gather over here." A dozen bracelets clank as Ms. Skyeblu waves her arms to get our attention. "There's got to be a logical reason for all this. Some short in the wiring, I would imagine."

Elbie dashes up to Ms. Skyeblu, his eyes wide. "I think the school got struck by lightning, and the whole building is on fire. Want me to pull the alarm for you?"

All heads turn to Miss Skyeblu.

"Oh, no you don't!" With the red plastic wall alarm only a few feet behind her, Ms. Skyeblu widens her stance, and, nostrils flaring, raises her arms like a basketball player trying to block a shot. "Back! Get back."

Defeated, Elbie trudges back to where I'm standing. "Dang," he mutters. "Ol' Hippy Crystal knows me better than I thought she did."

The lights seem to be staying on, and Ms. Skyeblu announces that we can continue searching for books. But now, it isn't the dark we're dealing with. There's a very cold breeze blowing through the room.

"Lucky me," Elbie says, fanning the cold air flowing out of the air conditioning vent above us. "I'm wearing shorts, and now the AC is jacked up too."

At least he has a sweatshirt. I remember seeing the temperature controller on the far wall during our other visits. "Some people may blame you for the lights, but they sure can't accuse you of messing with the air conditioning." I point. "See? It's locked behind a clear plastic cover."

Elbie's gaze follows my finger. "Okay, so, if this isn't just a prank, what do *you* think's causing it?"

Not knowing, I shrug and rub my bare arms as the cold breeze turns into a wind storm. Books standing on display tip over. Papers fly off of tables. Girls' hair whips into their faces. Expecting more screaming, I press my hands to my ears again.

Elbie shakes his head slowly as he zips his sweat jacket up to his neck. "Man, I have never felt AC *this* strong. I'm sure glad this place doesn't have ceiling sprinklers. If it did, we'd be soaked by now. Come on. Let's go sit down." He barely gets two steps before he falls to his knees, skidding to a stop on the rug.

I pull him to his feet. "You tripped over your laces again. Why don't you double-knot them?"

"I thought I did." Eyebrows gathered, Elbie rubs his knees, then kneels to triple-knot his laces. "Dawg, there is definitely something weird going on in this library."

Elbie is right. But I can't tell if it's the air-conditioning making the little hairs on my arms stand up, or a ghost.

We sit down just as Ms. Skyeblu lurches past us. She dashes behind the check-out counter and into her office, bright orange curls wild and bouncing. The small room has windows across the outside wall and door, so we can still see her, even after she closes the door. With the lights flashing on and off now, watching the librarian snatch up the phone and bang buttons is a lot like watching an old-time silent movie. She holds the receiver to her ear, then, after a few seconds of standing there open mouthed, slams it back on the holder.

Looks like the phone isn't working either.

Round-eyed and lipstick smeared, Ms. Skyeblu shuffles out of the office. Her curls bob as her head whips from side to side, gaping at so much madness.

"Ms. Skyeblu looks like she's watching a tennis match," I tell Elbie.

"Yeah. A real crazy tennis match."

As the lights continue to flash and the air continues to blow, our frazzled librarian grabs a wastebasket and darts around the library grabbing up papers and returning fallen books to their shelves.

Not sure of what to make of Ms. Skyeblu's expression, I uncover one ear and lean closer to Elbie so she won't hear me. "She's upset, isn't she?"

"Yeah, you could say that."

I look at Elbie's nice warm sweatshirt and hug myself, remembering my own jacket back in the classroom. "I wish Mr. Minelli would come get us," I tell Elbie. "Ms. Skyeblu is nice, but somebody needs to take control of this place."

"Okay, everyone quiet down!"

The lights snap back on for what seems to be the hundredth time, and all heads turn in the direction of the deep male voice. In the open doorway stands Mr. Nguyen, our principal. As usual, he's wearing a suit. It's shiny and black, a lot like his slicked-back hair.

"Finally," Elbie whispers. "Somebody who can straighten out this mess."

As if magically cued by Mr. Nguyen's voice, the air conditioner clicks off.

"How about Mr. Nguyen?" I ask Elbie. "Does *he* look upset?"

He elbows me in the ribs, one finger pressed to his lips.

"What? Am I talking too loudly again?"

Too late. My voice has attracted Mr. Nguyen's attention, and since Elbie is right beside me, it's him Mr. Nguyen focuses on.

"Elbie Bird . . ." he says in a menacing voice just above a whisper.

Elbie shrinks back a little. "Thanks a lot, Joey." He slips behind me and murmurs, "I bet this is how a mouse feels when a hawk flies over him."

Lucky for Elbie, Ms. Skyeblu distracts Mr. Nguyen by racing over to him, bracelets jangling. "Curtis, you should have been here. We were *soooo* freaked out." Her frizzed-out hair reminds me of the tumbleweeds in the cowboy movie Dad and I watched last night.

Elbie can't help but laugh. "Oh-my-god, Joey. Do you see what I see?"

"Of course, I do. The lights are back on now."

"Yeah, but it's not just her hair. Her face. It's . . . it's . . ."

"Disheveled?" I look at Elbie for three whole seconds. Not a record for anyone else, but for a kid with Asperger's Syndrome, not bad.

His shoulders sag. "Yeah, that's it."

"Should I have used a different word? Unkempt, maybe?" I take a harder look at Ms. Skyeblu, now deep in conversation with Principal Nguyen. Besides the messed-up hair, her lipstick has managed to smear itself halfway to her left ear. "No, there's no doubt about it, Elbie. That woman is extremely disheveled."

As everyone stares at the grownups, Mr. Nguyen flashes the class a smile, then steers Ms. Skyeblu out into the hallway. Maybe having so many eyes on him has made him uncomfortable. I know I would be. Hands on hips, he stands nose-to-nose with Ms. Skyeblu. I wonder if she can smell his breath.

This time Mr. Nguyen does all the talking while Ms. Skyeblu stands there, her hands constantly kneading as if she's washing them under an invisible faucet. Even though Mr. Nguyen is speaking quietly, I can still catch a few words. Madhouse is one of them. He also says lack of control three times, and something about her looking in a mirror. Finally, he runs out of words and she watches him leave, hands at her side, bracelets quiet.

For a while, she keeps her back to us all, and we watch and wait quietly. Then, Ms. Skyeblu steps back into the room. Her eyes are moist as she claps her hands three times.

"Okay, people." Her voice is different now. Smaller. "If you're holding books, please leave them on one of the tables and line up. I have an announcement to make." Her expression confuses me. The corners of her mouth are curved up, but her eyes are not happy.

"Does Ms. Skyeblu look sad to you?" I ask Elbie, this time remembering to whisper.

"Come on, man. You just saw Nguyen yelling at her."

"How was that yelling? I could barely hear him."

"Sometimes yelling doesn't have to be loud."

I study Ms. Skyeblu as the kids straggle toward the door. Now brimming with tears, her eyes gleam under the bright fluorescent lights. I didn't think it was possible, but Elbie is right. People really *can* yell quietly.

Once the class is lined up and silent, Ms. Skyeblu announces, "I know it's a major drag, but everyone has to go back to class now."

Like other people do when they're frustrated, I throw up my hand. "But I never got to check out *The Ultimate Bugopedia.*"

"I'm really sorry, Joey. But you saw how uptight Mr. Nguyen got. He wants everybody out. Now."

"Looks like that's all she wrote," Elbie says. "Sorry, man. I know how much you wanted to read that bug book."

He heads for the door, and I jog to catch up. "What's all she wrote? Are you talking about Ms. Skyeblu, because I never saw her—"

"No, man. It's just a figure of speech. It means the show's over. I could just as well have said Elvis has left the building."

"What show? Are you talking about Elvis Presley's ghost? Why didn't I see him? Was he wearing one of those sparkly outfits with the huge bell-bottom pants?"

Elbie gives me a familiar look that tells me I didn't get the joke. I shut my mouth. Fine. But I'll figure out how to get that bug book. Elvis has not left the building . . . yet.

CHAPTER 5

THE NEXT MORNING our teacher, Mr. Minelli, announces the library will remain closed until further notice.

"How long is that?" I ask him.

"Dunno. Might be a day . . . might be a month."

That long? "As you often say, that is unacceptable."

He chuckles. "Then I suggest you take your concerns to Mr. Nguyen."

Since I'd rather deal with Ms. Skyeblu than our principal, I formulate a different plan, and as soon as Mr. Minelli is distracted, I tap Elbie's shoulder. He turns around, his lips stretched into a wide grin. "You want me to go to the library with you during lunch recess, right?"

"How did you know?"

"Easy. Nothing comes between you and your creepie crawlies."

"That's very true. I just hope Ms. Skyeblu is still there."

I PULL THE library door open four hours later and immediately cough. Not only is the room cold and dark, but there's a hint of smoke in the air, which smells a bit like burning garbage. Determined to read that bug book, I push Elbie toward the check-out desk where Ms. Skyeblu, is repairing a torn book jacket by the light of a small electric camping lantern. Wrapped in a big afghan, she looks a lot like an old Native American woman sitting by a campfire.

"Is someone there?" She swivels her head toward us, and as Elbie steps into the light, her eyes narrow. Then, she sees I'm there too.

"Oh, hello, boys. Didn't you hear the announcement this morning? The library is closed."

This close to Ms. Skyeblu, the weird odor is even stronger. I reach up to hold my nose, but remember Theresa saying people might find that offensive. "We heard," I answer, "but I was hoping you might let me check out that bug book I was looking for yesterday. The new one, remember? The *Bugopedia.*"

"Oh, that's right." She tips her head tips to the side. "I'm sorry, Joey. I usually set the new insect books aside for you. Guess I forgot this time."

"That's okay. I know exactly where it is. If you let me borrow your flashlight, I'll get it right now."

"That's the thing." Ms. Skyeblu's face pinches as if remembering something unpleasant. "I've got a dentist appointment in fifteen minutes." She eyes Elbie as he continues to sniff the air. "But even if I didn't, no electricity means no computers. And without them, I can't check anything out, even to you, little buddy."

"That stinks," Elbie says. Seeing Ms. Skyeblu's eyebrows shoot up, he shakes his head. "I was talking about the computers being down, not the . . ." He takes a few more sniffs. "What is that, anyway?"

Clutching the blanket to her, Ms. Skyeblu steps back into her office and quickly returns carrying a bowl of rocks. On top, a small bunch of green twigs wrapped in string is giving off a thin curl of smoke. "It's sage," she tells us. "The smoke is supposed to cleanse away the bad energies."

With the air conditioning still blasting, Elbie rubs the goosebumps from his arms and smiles. "Guess it hasn't kicked in yet." That brings a sour look from Ms. Skyeblu, so he adds, "And that's a shame, because I know how much you enjoy your work."

"Yeah, right." Ms. Skyeblu shrugs off the afghan, leaving it in her chair. "Well, if I'm going to make that appointment I better get going."

"Wait. What if Joey checks that book out the old-school way?" Elbie taps the pad of orange sticky notes lying on the desk between them. "You could write the information down on one of these, then, when things are back to normal, you enter it into the computer and boom, we're all good."

"I guess that would work." Ms. Skyeblu frowns at her watch. "*If* I had the time, but I don't, so . . ." She tips her head toward the door.

I make myself look her in the eye and say, "I can write everything down myself. Please, Miss Skyeblu. We won't stay long. I promise."

Her eyes close to slits. "And do you promise Elbie won't do anything crazy while I'm gone?"

"Except for what I write on the sticky-note, you'll find no other evidence of us being here."

"I'm holding you to that." She digs two silver flashlights out of a drawer, passes one to me, but hesitates with the second.

"Oh, come on," Elbie says, slapping one hand over his heart. "Don't you think you're overreacting just a teeny tiny bit? You know I had nothing to do with the lights and air conditioning. I am *not* Jack the Ripper, and that flashlight you're handing me is *not* a butcher knife."

"Get real, Elbie. That might all be true, but your performance yesterday only made things worse. Libraries are supposed to be mellow, and that wasn't the first time you've upset the vibe in here." With what I can only describe as a soft grunt, she passes the second flashlight to Elbie, then slides the pad across the desk to me along with a pencil. "Just write down your name, the title of the book, and the author. And, Elbie, if you plan on checking out another book between now and the end of sixth grade, there better not be one thing out of place when I get back."

She carries the sage back into her office, and we watch through the glass as she slips on a suede jacket and picks up a large matching purse. Moments later, she's back at the checkout desk, reaching for the electric camping lamp. "I'm turning this off now, so click on your flashlights." Once we're ready, she heads for the door, then turns. "I don't want anyone sneaking in here while I'm gone, so I'm going to lock the door now. When you leave, please make sure you shut it."

"Not very mellow for a hippy," Elbie mutters once Ms. Skyeblu leaves.

"Well, what do you expect? Remember what Mr. Minnelli said about how people judge you by past interactions?"

"Yeah, yeah. Come on. We don't have a lot of time." He snaps on his flashlight and yanks me into the shadows. "If she didn't already hate me so much I'd borrow that blanket. It's freezing in here." He rubs his arms as I kneel down in front of the insect section.

After a couple of minutes, I frown up at Elbie. "I can't find it."

"Let me look." Crouching alongside me, he rescans the entire shelf with his own flashlight. "Maybe ol' Miss Tie-dye forgot she already checked it out to somebody else."

"Impossible. She knows how much I love reading about insects."

"Well, maybe some kid thought it would be funny to stick it on the wrong shelf somewhere."

I look at Elbie sideways. "Do I know this person?"

"What? Oh, heck no. I would never do that. At least not to you. And never for more than thirty seconds. Sixty, tops."

"Then where is it?"

On the far side of the room, something goes thunk, and like two meercats, we straighten and peer into the darkness.

"That sounded like a book falling onto the floor," I whisper. "Ms. Skyeblu? Are you back?"

Nothing.

Elbie shines his flashlight onto the big wall clock across the room. "Recess is going to end soon. Maybe we should head back to class."

"Not until I check out that bug book."

"Okay, you keep looking, but I'm going to figure out what that noise was. The last thing I need is that hippy woman exiling me for life because some earthquake tremor knocked *Frog and Toad* off its shelf."

Elbie's back a few seconds later, a dog-eared hardback clutched in one hand. "Well, that was weird."

"What? It really was *Frog and Toad* we heard fall?"

"No, but I found this: *Stolen Treasure*. It was lying on the floor, in the middle of the D to H section."

"Okay, so find the shelf it fell from and put it back."

"That's the thing. The author's last name is Quincy, but the Qs are way over on the other—"

Thunk.

This one sounds like it's right behind us.

Wondering how I'm supposed to find my book with all these interruptions, I jog around to the other side of the shelf and discover another hardback lying on the rug. The title of this one is *Betrayed.* "We are definitely not dealing with earthquake tremors," I tell Elbie as we shine our flashlights around the room. "I think there's a ghost in here."

"In a library?" Elbie's lips pucker.

"Why not? It would certainly explain all that crazy stuff yesterday. And *Betrayed* is in the wrong part of the library, just like *Stolen Treasure* was. Ms. Skyeblu would never display a fiction book in the non-fiction section."

"True, for a hippy, she is pretty obsessive. But if a ghost is responsible for all this weird stuff, then, where's it getting the energy from? Both flashlights are working fine, and it can't be from the air. The room's way too cold for that."

"Maybe it learned how to tap into the electrical wires. That would explain its control of the lights and air-conditioning." I call out, "If there's really a ghost in here, please do that again."

Seconds later, we hear something hit the floor, this time back where I was searching for the bug book. We turn around just as another hardcover sails over the shelves. Without a word, we race over and find two books lying side by side on the carpet. I recognize one immediately. It's my favorite bug book, *Poisonous Spiders of the World.* The title of the other book is *Hostage.*

We each pick up one and shine our flashlights around the library.

"Want to hear what I think?" Elbie says.

"Not being psychic, it's the only way I'll ever find out."

He lets out a sigh, then says, "I think the ghost is using the titles of these books to communicate with us."

"Interesting." We place the four hardbacks side by side on a nearby table. "*Betrayed, Stolen Treasure, Hostage,* and *Poisonous Spiders of the World.*" I tip back my head and call out to the room, "Were you betrayed when somebody held you hostage, and then they murdered you with the venom of a Brazilian Wandering Spider?"

"Seriously?" Elbie whispers. "That's the best you can come up with?"

"Why not? Of all the spiders in the world, the Brazilian Wandering Spider is considered the most poisonous." I notice Elbie looking at me like I'm wearing my underwear on the outside and shrug. "What? I don't hear you coming up with any suggestions."

Brrrrreeeeeeeezzzzzzzzzzz!

A few feet away, the newly installed bell, a cross between a firetruck siren and the buzz of a school bus-sized mosquito, goes off. Startled, we both cry out. Elbie grabs his chest, but I grab my ears, and the brain-stabbing racket goes on for three long seconds.

"I will never get used to that," Elbie says, once the torture has ended.

Still wincing, I say, "Let's go back to class. We can talk to the ghost later."

As promised, we put away the books and leave the flashlights on Ms. Skyeblu's desk before heading for the exit. Compared to the cave-like library, the hallway is blinding. I blink hard to adjust my pupils as Elbie tugs the door shut.

"Check it," I tell him.

He jiggles the knob, and once we're satisfied the library is secure, we turn to go just in time for both of us to slam into Mr. Nguyen, who smells a little like cooking oil. Probaby because he always supervises the cafeteria during upper grade lunch.

"Why were you in the library?" he asks, pushing us off him. "He peers through the narrow window slit into the pitch-black room. "I don't see Ms. Skyeblu."

"Oh, she's there," Elbie says. "In the media room."

I look at him. "She is? I thought she went to her dentist appointment."

Elbie chuckles, then clears his throat. "Oh, that's right. I forgot. Miss Skyeblu did say something about an appointment. But before she left, she gave us permission to search for a book Joey needs."

"Really? Well, she shouldn't have left you unsupervised." Like Miss Skyeblu, Mr. Nguyen studies Elbie. "You sure everything is in order? No little . . . accidents?"

"All the books are in their places," I assure him. "The ghost tossed four of them on the floor, but we reshelved them."

"A haunted library, huh? That sounds like something Elbie would come up with." Nguyen peers down his nose at me. "Wait, didn't your sister win that ghost video contest last year. How much did she get? Two hundred thousand dollars?"

"Well, yes and no. My sister's friend Kerry got half, and a lot of it went to taxes, so . . ."

Nguyen makes a tsking sound with his tongue. "Yes, well, people believe anything these days. Go on, get to class."

"We're going," Elbie says.

But I have one more question. "Mr. Nguyen, do you know if anyone died in this library?"

"What kind of question is that? Get to class before I give you both detention."

CHAPTER 6

AFTER SCHOOL, ELBIE and I walk to the bike rack. "If no one died there," I say, thinking out loud, "then that ghost must have some other reason for haunting the library."

"I saw something like this in a scary movie once," Elbie says. "This family had all sorts of poltergeist problems, and it turned out their house was built on top of a Native American burial ground."

I look back at the red brick building behind me. "But Fern Creek Elementary was built more than fifty years ago. If that was true, why would the ghosts wait so long to get upset?"

"Good point." Elbie removes the lock from his bike and zips it into his pack. "Okay, so maybe this is a homeless ghost, and on its travels, it just happened to stop at our school."

"I guess that's possible. But whoever it is, they seem very ticked off about something."

"You got that right. But if we're going to figure out all the whats and whys, we need a name, dawg. We don't even know if that ghost is a man or a woman."

I spin the combination on my own lock. "My sister's pretty good at those things. Maybe she can help us."

"Smart idea. Let's go to your house and tell Theresa what happened."

"We can't. She and Kerry are at the town library this afternoon. They're working on some sort of school project."

Elbie clicks on his helmet and climbs onto his bike. "Actually, the library sounds like a smart place to start. It's closer to my house than yours. Come home with me. You can call your dad from there and ask if it's okay to ride over."

"All right." I point at his shoes. "But tie your laces. They could get caught in your bike spokes."

SINCE WE'RE BOTH riding bicycles, we enter the mortuary property through the back alley.

"Just drop your bike anywhere," Elbie says. He hops off his own and races up the backstairs to the second floor, leaving the green BMX lying the middle of the wide driveway, front wheel spinning.

In no such rush, I find a shady spot under the carport in front of their big stretch limo, drop the kickstand, and check its stability before following Elbie up to the family's living area on the second floor.

After shouting his parents' name and getting no answers, Elbie discovers a note on the kitchen table. "My dad's working and my mom's out shopping," he tells me. "Hurry up and call your house, then we'll go find my dad."

As I push the phone's buttons, Elbie's cat pads silently into the kitchen, stretches, then strolls over, sits at my feet, and stares up at me. I stare back, waiting for Skunky to rub up against me or possibly bite my ankle.

"I think he hates me," I say, keeping my eye on the cat as I wait for my dad to pick up the phone.

"That's crazy."

As if proving me right, Skunky bites onto one of my pant legs and pulls. The cat's claws click against the ceramic tile floor as he leans back, putting his weight into it.

I ignore Skunky's attack, and eventually, Dad answers the phone. After a few words back and forth, I hang up. "He says since Theresa's already at the library, it's okay."

"Good," Elbie says. He looks up at Mrs. Bird's owl-shaped wall clock. "Dad's probably in the basement. We'll stop in the lobby on the way down. There's something I want to show you."

He shoos Skunky away for me, and we head downstairs. As always, the scents of past funerals crowd my nostrils.

Roses, carnations, daffodils, a thousand times nicer than Miss Skyeblu's stinky old sage. As we reach the bottom of the stairs, the smell gets stronger. The chapel doors are open, and the sign outside tells me Mr. Prendergast's services will be starting in about an hour. Beside the sign stands the guestbook pedestal, and on top, a lavender colored book and matching pen. Inside, a lot of really pretty flower arrangements line the back wall, two shaped like giant horseshoes. In the center of it all rests Mr. Prendergast's bright purple casket. Like his ghost, his body is dressed in jockey silks.

"I'd rather not go in there," I tell Elbie. "It . . . it reminds me too much of . . . you know."

"Oh, sorry, man. I didn't think of that. Your mom's only been gone a year, huh?"

"Sixteen months and twelve days."

"Well, let me show you this one thing. You'll like it, and you don't have to go into the chapel."

"This isn't another trick, is it?"

He grins. "No, I swear. Remember I promised to do something for Mr. P if he scared you? Watch what happens when I walk inside."

Still a little wary, I stand by the guestbook pedestal. As Elbie steps into the chapel, a trumpet blares.

Ta ta ta tatara, tatara, ta ta ta tuuuum.

"Pretty cool, huh?" Elbie points out a small device attached to the chapel's doorframe. "And it was cheap too. All we had to buy was that garage door sensor. We already had the speakers."

"Isn't that the music they play at horseracing tracks right before the start of each race?"

"Yup, just what Mr. P asked for."

As I glance back at the casket, Elbie's horn goes off again.

Ta ta ta tatara, tatara, ta ta ta tuuuuuuum.

"I think your dad needs to make some adjustments," I tell Elbie. "Nobody went in there."

"But someone came out!" The raspy voice in my ear makes me jump. It's Mr. Prendergast, bringing with him a horsy smell and an icy chill. "Sorry, kid. Couldn't resist it." He looks at Elbie with his squinty forgot-his-sunglasses grin. "Thanks for the trumpet, Elbie. My buddies are going to love it." With a tip of his purple jockey cap, the ghost dissolves into the nearby air conditioning vent.

Once the cold patch of air caused by Mr. Prendergast's appearance fades, I say, "If he has a lot of friends, it's going to be very noisy in here."

"Dad said the same thing, but Mr. P didn't care. It's his favorite sound in the whole world, and since he's not going to be hearing it anymore . . ."

"I get it, but I'm still glad I'm not going to be here."

"Let the grownups worry about that. Let's go find my dad. He needs to know where we're going."

He high steps over the invisible beam, and we head down the hallway past the casket room. "Feel like trying one of them out *today*?"

Since he asks me that every time I come over, I say, "No, thank you," and continue past to the basement door.

"You down there, Dad?" Elbie calls, although not very loudly.

"Maybe he stepped out for a while."

"No way," Elbie says. "Mr. P's services start in an hour."

At the bottom of the concrete steps, Elbie makes a right into the dimly lit embalming room. My chest immediately tightens.

"I'll just wait here," I whisper.

"What? Why? I know there's a body in there, but he's covered with a sheet. Come and say hi to my dad. He's probably in the back."

"Oh, all right." I gather my courage and step into the embalming room. Like the last time we came down here, the smell of formaldehyde is faint, but I hate it just the same. Elbie's right about the body. Covered from his head to his ankles, all I can see are two big feet. Nothing scary, especially since they're covered with blue and yellow Warriors socks. There's a small metal tray-table nearby. On top are two little brown plastic things.

Noticing my hands are knotted into fists, I force them open. I'll be fine, I tell myself. Unlike the statues in Madame Tussaud's Wax Museum, this body's not standing up.

"Come on," Elbie says. "There's another storage room back behind the refrigerator unit. He's probably there."

Since Elbie will think I'm afraid if I refuse, I follow him into the room. "You said your dad always puts the bodies on snow when he isn't working on them," I say, eyes glued to the black and white checkered floor tiles.

"Not snow, ice. And you're right. Now who could this be? Want to see?" I look up as Elbie reaches for the sheet.

"No, thanks." I grab his wrist and pull him toward me. "Can we *please* find your dad now?"

"Oh, yeah, sure." Elbie turns and faces the dark hallway next to the refrigerators, tips back his head, and calls out, "Da-aaad!"

As he yells his father's name, the shape on the table shudders.

"Uh . . . Elbie?" I stumble back against the tray table, which rolls across the room as the dead body rises onto its elbows. This is not supposed to happen. My heart batters away in my chest as one chocolate-brown hand reaches out from beneath the sheet and slides it off of its face.

Elbie's dad swings his legs over the side of the table and sits up. "Linwood Bartholomew Bird, why the heck are you yelling?"

Realizing I've been holding my breath, I fill my lungs, drawing in the familiar eucalyptus scent I've come to associate with the man. Linwood Bartholomew? So, that's why they call him Elbie. Linwood Bartholomew . . . L. B.

Elbie tries to explain his shouting, but his dad just points at the tray table. "My hearing aids. Pass them over." Wearing only a white dress shirt and plaid boxer shorts, he holds one hand out, palm up.

Oh, so that's what those little plastic things are.

Once his dad has them on, Elbie starts over. "I didn't know that was you, Dad. I-I thought it was just another—"

"Another body? Really son?" Mr. Bird hops off the table and flips on the ceiling lights. He then strides over to the nearby clothes rack where a lone pair of dark blue slacks hang.

"Why did you take your pants off?" I ask him.

"It's a trick my daddy taught me. Keeps them from wrinkling while I nap." As Mr. Bird steps into his pants, he glares at Elbie. "Boy, I've been napping on these tables ever since you learned to walk. Guess you suddenly forgot all about my back problems, huh?" He swats Elbie's butt. "Go on, bring me my coat and tie."

The matching dark blue jacket is hanging on the back of a nearby folding chair along with a gray tie, already knotted. Elbie snatches them up and holds the jacket for his father to slip on.

As Mr. Bird dresses, he glances at the wall clock, then at Elbie. "It's a good thing you got me up. Looks like I forgot to set the alarm." He loops the necktie over his head, then looks at me, one side of his mouth curved upward. "Sorry if I scared you, Joey."

"It wasn't your fault. It was Linwood Bartholomew's."

"Arrrgggg!" Elbie turns toward me, palms pressed together. "Please, *please*, don't call me that. It's bad enough when my parents say it."

"Linwood and Bartholomew. Those are very unusual names."

"He can blame both his granddaddies for them," Mr. Bird says, herding us out of the room and toward the stairs. "Now . . . besides using me to scare Joey half to death, was there some other reason you came down here?"

CHAPTER 7

AFTER ELBIE APOLOGIZES five different ways, Mr. Bird gives him permission to go to the library with me, and five minutes later we're pulling open the huge wooden double doors of the hundred-and-something-year-old building. The inside smells like old books, mold, and the same cinnamon-scented room freshener my mom used to buy. The check-out desk is straight ahead, surrounded by a wide carpeted walkway. There are six wooden tables on either side. Beyond, several tall shelves block our view of the far wall.

"Is that Theresa?" Elbie whispers. He points his chin at a brown-haired girl seated at one of the far tables in the non-fiction section. Even though I'm too far away to smell her coconut-scented shampoo, I recognize my thirteen-year-old sister immediately.

"How come her hair is curly and yours and your dad's are straight?" Elbie asks as we stride over.

"Because she takes after my mom."

"Oh, I get it." Elbie holds up his hand, gesturing for me to stop. I do, and he leans toward me. "You know, your sister is just perfect for a *Creep and Freak*. Why don't *you* do it? My present for scaring you back at the house."

I shake my head. "You go ahead. Scaring people isn't my cup of teeth."

Elbie chuckles. "That's tea."

"Whatever." I wave him forward. "Just don't blame me if you get punched."

Engrossed in cleaning her glasses, Theresa doesn't seem to notice Elbie creeping up behind her. As he closes in, he gives me a quick wink, raises his hands, and wiggles his fingers. But just as he's about to touch her, I smell the slightest hint of pineapples, and someone leaps out from behind the nearest bookcase and grabs Elbie's shoulders, making him shriek. It's Kerry, Theresa's ghost-chasing partner and best buddy.

"Holy crabs!" a bug-eyed Theresa shouts. She leaps up from her chair, knocking it on its side. In the next aisle, two little girls scream and hug each other.

Seeing all this, Kerry doubles over in a near-silent laugh, both hands pressed to her mouth. At six-two, she's much taller than any eighth graders I've seen. With Elbie shorter than me and Theresa just three inches taller than my four-feet-eleven inches, the contrast is huge. If we were animals in a petting zoo, Kerry would be the llama and the rest of us would be the baby goats.

With all the racket we've been making, it isn't long before a pudgy little security guard with thinning hair storms across the library toward us. The others don't see him coming, but I can't help but stare, because for a short man, he takes very long strides.

"What's going on here?" the guard barks, startling everyone but me.

As usual, Elbie doesn't stay flustered long. "We saw a rat," he shouts, turning any head that isn't already watching.

Really? Where?

Before I can ask, Elbie bursts out with, "It was right there, and it was huge."

Although the look on his face would better suit someone talking about an escaped velociraptor, he points at the top of the nearest bookcase, then looks to Kerry, who stares down at him with her brown and green mismatched eyes, both brows raised to their limit.

"That's right," she finally sputters, exaggerating her British accent. "Bloody terrifying! Someone needs to catch that creature. It was this big."

I blink hard, amazed how far apart Kerry is holding her hands. That is one massive rat. But what's it doing in a library?

Like me, the guard peers up at the bookcase in question. "I don't see anything," he says, echoing my thoughts.

"Ugh!" Kerry looms over the little man, hands on hips. "Did you expect it to pose for a photo?"

"Well?" Theresa says, taking the same stance as Kerry.

"Nuh, no . . ." The guard backs up, suddenly red cheeked. He fumbles a pad and pen from his front shirt pocket, but before he can write anything down, Elbie shouts again, making us all jump.

"There it goes!" He stabs his finger in the direction of the two little girls who have been watching his performance the whole time. Squealing, they stumble over each other as they rush for the exit.

Kerry pushes the guard in their direction. "Hurry! Before that monster bites them."

"Oh, gee." The guard pockets his notepad and jogs after the girls.

With the guard gone, Kerry confuses me even more by giving Elbie a high-five. "You cheeky little hound." How do you come up with this stuff?"

Theresa stands her chair up and looks from Elbie to Kerry. "Him? What about you?" She flaps her hands in front of her face. "Oh, a monster. Bloody terrifying." Noticing me, she peers over the top of her constantly-smudged lenses and smiles. "Hey, little brother. What are you and this drama queen doing here? Did Mr. Minelli assign you another science report?"

"No. We were looking for you two."

Elbie throws his chest out. "We found you another ghost."

At the sound of the G-word, Kerry's eyes sparkle, and she gives Elbie a shove. "Get out. Where?"

"In our school library," he says, stumbling backward. "The ceiling lights keep going on and off and the air conditioner blasts all over the place. The principal won't let any more classes in there until the maintenance men can figure out what's wrong with it."

Kerry narrows her eyes. "So what makes you think it's not simply an electrical problem?"

This time I answer. "Because when I talked Ms. Skyeblu into letting us look for the new bug book, other books started falling off the shelves. But most importantly, we couldn't locate *The Ultimate Bugopedia*. My theory is that the book is being held for ransom by the ghost. It wants us to help it do something."

"Good one," Elbie says. "That makes tons more sense than your first theory."

Theresa looks back and forth between us. "What's all this about theories? You mean it didn't talk to you?"

"I *wish*," Elbie says." That would have been sooooooo much easier."

"It communicated with book titles," I explain. "First it threw down one called *Betrayed,* then *Stolen Treasure, Ransom,* and *Poisonous Spiders of the World.*"

The girls look at each other and nod. I knew they'd get it.

"Smart ghost," Kerry says, "but what can *we* do? I doubt that principal of yours will allow us access, especially if we plan on using our equipment."

"That's okay," Elbie says. "We aren't looking for that kind of help now, anyway. What we need is information. We don't even know who the ghost is. Since it hangs out in our school library, we thought you could help us find out if someone died there. You know, like in old newspapers and stuff."

"Sure, we can teach you how to use the microfiche," Kerry says.

"What's a microfiche?" Elbie asks.

"It's a lot like a photo negative," Theresa says.

Elbie and I look at each other, so she adds, "It's a miniature copy of a newspaper page, but on transparent plastic rectangles a little bigger than your hand. Back before we had computers, if you wanted to read an old newspaper you would stick the microfiche into a machine and it would magnify it. There's one here at the library but using that old thing could take forever." She pauses a few moments, then turns to Elbie. "How about this? You help Kerry with our homework project, and Joey and I will see what we can find online."

THE LIBRARY'S COMPUTERS are set up on a long table in a back room, three on one side, three on the other. There's a high school-aged boy sitting at one, and two seats over, a man about Dad's age. We move to the empty side where Theresa sets me down in front of the middle computer, then drags a chair up beside me.

"Okay, type in Fern Creek Elementary," she tells me.

A long list of links pops up.

"What are these?" I ask her, pointing at the first few.

"Those look like review websites. You type in your school's name and it tells you if it's good or not."

"I didn't even know those exist. Want to try one?"

"You can do that at home. What we're looking for is news." Theresa cleans her glasses on her shirt, then scans the top of the screen with her pointer finger. "See? Images, videos, maps, news, and explore. Click on news."

I do, and a list appears on the screen. "All of these articles are about Open Houses and Back to School Nights. There's nothing about anyone dying there."

"Well, maybe the ghost didn't die on campus. Maybe your library is just someplace they really liked being when they were alive."

"I guess that's possible. I'm going to search Fern Creek Elementary Library this time."

The results show two articles about book fairs and one about some children's book author who came to read to the kindergarten class. I scroll down, and finding nothing better, click on the one about the author. A photo of a woman sitting in Ms. Skyeblu's reading rocker pops up. A bunch of little kids are sitting on the floor in front of her. The woman is pencil thin with tar-black hair and she's showing them a book with pictures of zoo animals. Standing alongside her is a heavyset grandma-type lady I don't recognize.

"This is five-years-old," Theresa says. She reads the caption aloud. "Local children's author, Margaret Early, enthralls kindergarteners with her latest picture book, *Me, Monkeys, and Mikey.*"

"Okay, so how do we find out if she's the ghost?"

"Let's search the name and see what comes up."

Thirty seconds later we learn Margaret Early is still alive and will be signing books over in Brimley next Saturday.

Theresa sits back in her chair. "Obviously, Margaret isn't our ghost. Maybe we do have to try the microfiche. If that ghost died a long time ago, the Internet probably isn't going to do us any good since news has only been available online for a few years."

"How about the other lady?" I tap the screen. "Couldn't *she* be the ghost?"

"I suppose. Do you know who she is?"

"No, I haven't seen her before. Ugh! I think I'm never going to read that bug book."

Theresa pushes out her chair and stands. "You know, the Internet doesn't have all the answers. Just print out the picture and take it to school tomorrow. Mr. Minelli's been teaching there a long time, so there's a good chance he was around when that photo was taken."

I hit the print page button and race over to the ancient printer as a hazy black and white image spills out onto the plastic tray. "It's not exactly high definition."

"No, but good enough for your teacher to recognize who she is. Let's go show the others."

CHAPTER 8

SINCE MR. MINELLI is always super busy during the first part of the day, Elbie and I wait for morning recess and follow him out to the playground so we can talk while he supervises the grade four to six kids. Like every other day, he smells good. Fresh, like oranges rolled in baby powder. He recognizes the woman as soon as I unfold the printout.

"That's Sylvia Cowan. She was our librarian a few years back."

"So why doesn't she work here anymore?" Elbie asks. "She retire?"

Mr. Minelli's thin lips twist to the side. "Uh, sort of."

"Sort of?" I shake my head. "How does a person *sort of* retire?"

"Well," Mr. Minelli turns his large, ex-football player body to watch some boys playing tetherball, "ever since I was a kid, she ran that library. A sweet woman, but tough. Kind of a grandma/drill sergeant. Then one day, she was just gone."

"Did you ever find out what happened to her?" Elbie asks.

Mr. Minelli shouts at a girl to stop climbing up the slide backward, then considers Elbie's question. After a few moments, he say, "Mr. Nguyen announced her leaving to the staff, but said he wasn't allowed to talk about it. Something to do with her being involved in some legal matters. That was three years ago. They hired another librarian, but her husband was in the air force, and they moved to Germany a year later. That's when Ms. Skyeblu got the job."

"But what were Sylvia Cowan's legal matters?" I ask him. "And where did she go?"

"That, I don't know." He tucks his whistle between his lips, and I cover my ears while he blows hard, one long thick finger pointing at a group of boys arguing over a big red ball. "Sorry, guys, but I better break that up." He starts to walk away, then turns back to Elbie, one corner of his mouth curved upward. "By the way, kiddo, your fly is open."

"Well, at least we know her name now," I tell Elbie as he fumbles to zip his pants. "Why don't you come over to my house after school? We can Google Sylvia Cowan there."

"Sure, I'll call my—"

The ear-piercing buzz of the school bell makes us both jump, and I cover my ears as fast as possible. Elbie's reaction is stronger.

"Geez, Louise!" he wails. "Why does that thing always have to go off when I'm standing right next to it?"

"I don't know," I tell him. And how would I?

AFTER SCHOOL, WE ride our bikes straight to my house and run up to my room. But with not one single article about Sylvia Cowan, the Internet is no help. I close my laptop. "*Now* what are we going to do? I want that bug book."

Elbie reaches out his hand. "Let me see that photocopy again."

I unfold the paper and he studies the photo, eyes all squinty like that old jockey, Mr. Prendergast.

"Yeah . . . I remember now. We cremated her last week."

What? Why didn't you say that when I showed you the picture yesterday?"

"Heck, I don't know. That's an old picture, and when I saw her, she was lying down. People look different lying down. Especially when their eyes are closed."

"If Sylvia Cowan is our ghost, then you should know something about her."

"Oh, heck no. My dad's the one who deals with that stuff."

I spring from my chair. "Okay, then let's go ask him. I'll tell my dad we're going out again."

We run out into the hall and down the big staircase. At the bottom, we loop to the right, passing through the living room and into another hallway. This one leads to the kitchen, the dining room, and my dad's office. As I expect, he's busy writing another of his historical novels. It's his sixth and the second book since we moved into my grandmother's old Victorian, and we've only been here a little over a year. Since I don't have much homework, he says I can go to Elbie's, but I have to be back before dinner. We head to the foyer to get our bike helmets, and as I'm passing Elbie, Theresa opens the front door.

"Where are you guys off to in such a hurry?" she asks.

Kerry is right behind her. "Hi, guys. Did you learn anything about that librarian woman?"

"That's what we're doing right now," I tell her. "We're headed over to Elbie's house to ask his dad about her."

Elbie bumps his forehead with the heel of his hand. "I just realized we buried her last week."

"She's dead?" Kerry's gaze swivels from Elbie to me, then back again.

"Uh huh." Elbie gives Kerry one of his big Tic Tac smiles. "Want to come along?"

"To a mortuary?" Theresa's nose crinkles. "No, thank you."

"I'll pass too," Kerry says. "You boys have fun."

As the girls head up the stairs, I reach for the door, but Elbie blocks me. "I'm confused," he says, a bit louder than necessary. "I thought you said Kerry likes ghosts."

Halfway up, Kerry turns around. "You've got ghosts there?"

"All kinds of them. Black, white, old, young. But if you're not interested . . ."

"We're interested." She grabs Theresa's hand and pulls her back out onto the big front porch.

"Kerry, stop." Theresa's face looks like she's been sucking on a lemon. "Maybe you like ghosts, but I've seen more than I—"

"Oh, belt up. If I go, you go."

CHAPTER 9

FIVE MINUTES LATER, the four of us are parking our bikes behind The Virtue Funeral Home. Elbie leads us up the stairs to the living area where the scents of cinnamon, sugar, and vanilla tell me Mrs. Bird is baking again. Most likely, snickerdoodles. A large woman with straight shoulder-length black hair, we find her sitting at the kitchen table ordering caskets on her laptop. I'm right about the snickerdoodles. There's a plate of them next to the laptop, and more baking in the oven. After some introductions, she offers us each a cookie. Since Theresa is all into cooking, she immediately asks Mrs. Bird about the ingredients she used. While they're talking, Elbie pulls me aside.

"Hey, man," Elbie whispers, "I know you aren't into hanging with dead people, but all the bodies are put away, so don't sweat this."

I raise my arm and check my shirt for stains. "I'm not, but I really can't control that. Are you worried because you're feeling sweaty?"

His eyes squeeze shut for a moment. "All I'm asking is that you keep your mouth shut when we go down to the embalming room. You chill?"

Chill? I have no experience with the word used this way. Cool, yes. When not referring to temperature, it can mean good or amazing, but is chill the same thing? Unsure how to reply, I don't move as he reaches out with one closed hand.

"Come on, knuckle-bump."

Since that's something I do understand, I tap my fist against his, but I'm still not sure what he's trying to tell me. Behind us, Mrs. Bird and Theresa decide to share recipes, and the rest of us finish eating our cookies while they exchange email addresses.

"Where's Dad?" Elbie asks Mrs. Bird.

"I don't know. Probably in his office. If he's not there, then check the basement."

Even if Elbie's right, and all the bodies really are put away, I still hope we find Mr. Bird in his office. The less embalming fluid I smell, the better.

Once emails have been exchanged, we all thank Mrs. Bird for the cookies, and Elbie leads us downstairs to the lobby.

"Pretty dead today," he tells us.

"Ha ha," Theresa says. "That joke's so old it's got dust on it." She crosses her arms. I can't tell if she's cold or nervous about being here, but the temperature is fine for me, so I'm going with nervous.

Kerry scans the empty lobby, then peeks into the chapel, which is dark since there's no body on display. "Well, I haven't seen any ghosts yet. When do they come out?"

Elbie's normally easy-going face turns stern. "Don't let my dad hear you say that. This is a mortuary, not a carnival ride. The ghosts will show themselves *when* and *if* they feel like showing themselves. And even then, most people can't see them."

"Yeah, tell me about it." Kerry stamps her foot. "I wish I had my infrared camera with me. Things would be so much easier if I was like you three. All you need are your eyes."

"Well," Elbie smiles again, "you can always come back another day. If there's something we never run out of, it's ghosts."

The girls follow Elbie toward the hall, but I hang back, staring into the chapel. Something has changed. Even though there are no flowers there today, the scent is suddenly powerful, even from out here in the lobby. Do flowers have ghosts too?

The hairs on the back of my neck start to prickle. Someone is sitting in the front row. A dark shape. From this angle, I can't even tell if it's a man or a woman. If I mention it to Kerry, she'll only get ticked off for not having her equipment with her, so I stay quiet and soon, the figure vanishes.

"What's so interesting?" Kerry steps up beside me. "Did you see something?"

I pick my words carefully and say, "I always see something when my eyes are open. Unless, of course, it's night time and—"

"You know what I meant, Jojo. You saw a ghost, didn't you?"

"Only for a few seconds."

"Arg! And to think my gran once told me I would have a knack for it. A lot she knew."

Not sure what to say, I stare at my shoes, and after a moment, the others come back to get us.

"Come on," Elbie says. "The office is this way."

We follow Elbie down the hallway, first Kerry, then Theresa, then me. Since Kerry's a foot taller than Theresa, I can see her head keeps turning from side to side. I realize she's still looking for ghosts and can't help but smile. I hope she sees one.

Since Theresa still has her arms crossed high, I say, "Want to wear my sweatshirt?" as I step up beside her.

"Why do you ask that?"

"I thought you might be cold."

"Why would I be . . . ?" She drops her arms. "Thanks, but—except for the fact that I'm walking around in a mortuary—I'm fine."

Elbie points out his dad's disappointingly empty office, then steps to the door on the opposite wall. "This here's the casket room." He reaches around the corner and flicks on the light to reveal a dozen shiny caskets, each different from the next. "Anybody want to try one on for size?"

"Is he crazy?" Theresa asks me.

"I'm starting to think so."

After a few failed tries to convince us, he walks to the end of the hall and opens the door marked *PRIVATE*. This time, the downstairs lights are already on.

"Looks like he *is* down there. Ladies first," Elbie tells the girls.

Theresa and Kerry walk down the steps, and while neither girl is looking, Elbie presses one finger to his lips and closes one eye.

"What's wrong with your eye?" I ask.

"Nothing, I was . . ." He sighs and trots down the stairs.

Kerry must notice, because she asks us if everything is all right.

"I think he may have something in his eye," I answer.

"Trust me," Elbie says. "My eyes are fine. Let's go find my dad."

The girls edge past the stack of plastic-wrapped caskets, their heads turning in all directions. Just like the last time we were down there, the dimly lit embalming room is empty except for the sheet covered body on one of the tables.

My pulse races until I notice it's wearing yellow and blue socks. "Hey, isn't that—?"

"A dead body? It sure is. Dead. Very dead." Elbie turns to Kerry and Theresa, eyebrows raised. "I am so sorry. You probably don't want to see this."

"Definitely not," Theresa says, her face suddenly gone pale.

"But if we leave," Elbie's voice becomes a whisper, "you'll miss seeing his ghost."

"I can live with that," Theresa says.

She starts to leave, but before she can reach the door, Kerry tugs her back to Elbie and me.

"What was that about missing a ghost?" Kerry asks Elbie.

"All I'm saying is that ghosts usually stick around their body when it's being worked on." Elbie glances over his shoulder at the silent form behind him. "And this guy definitely needs more work."

Since Mrs. Bird probably isn't the only person to own Warriors socks, I search for more evidence, which I find easily. To my right, Mr. Bird's suitcoat and slacks are hanging on the nearby rack. If that's not enough, inches from the body's right hand is the metal tray table holding two tiny brown hearing aids. Yes, that is definitely Mr. Bird under that sheet, and I'll be very surprised if he's dead.

As I consider whether I should tell the girls, Theresa says, "Why not wait upstairs, Kerry? Even if the ghost does come, you won't see it."

Kerry shrugs. "Yeah, but I'm curious. We've never seen one so . . . so . . ."

"Recently passed?" Elbie says.

"Exactly. They're supposed to be super clear, right?" She looks at Theresa. "It would be brilliant to see it myself, but I'll be satisfied with a detailed description."

"Fine, fine." Arms crossed, Theresa turns to Elbie. "Is . . . is your dad really going to work on this body?"

"Uhhhhhhh . . ." Elbie looks his sheet-draped father up and down. "Except for the shoes, I'm guessing this guy's fully dressed, but he probably needs a little make-up. Joey, the ghosts like you more than me. Why don't *you* call this one?"

"Me? You said ghosts only come when they feel like it."

Theresa looks toward the back storeroom, then the stairs. "What about your dad? Shouldn't we go find him?"

"Oh, he'll pop up any minute. I guarantee it." Elbie glances around then turns to me. "Come on, Jojo, call the ghost. It'll be fun."

I look across the table at Kerry. Like other times, the thrill of a paranormal experience has caused her asthma to kick in. But even as she puffs on her inhaler, her mismatched eyes continue to sparkle. Nothing makes Kerry happier. In contrast, my big sister looks like she may throw up. No,

Theresa is not going to enjoy Elbie's prank. And neither will Mr. Bird.

As I consider my options, Elbie, all smiles, signals for us to come closer. "Stand right here," he tells Kerry and Theresa. "Ghosts like to hang out near the top end of their body."

Eyes bright and shiny, Kerry pulls Theresa along, stopping next to Mr. Bird's head. I position myself on the opposite side.

"Go on," Elbie says. "Call him."

I nod and say, "Hello, Mr. Bir—"

"Burbelson!" Elbie blurts. Chuckling, he looks back and forth between the girls. "His name's Frederick Burbelson. And say it loud, Jojo. He's deaf, remember?"

With Kerry standing between her and the body, Theresa leans out and whispers, "You've already met this guy?"

Since "this guy" is really Elbie's dad, I nod and stand there, unsure how to proceed. Don't be afraid," I say, more for Theresa and Mr. Bird's benefit than any ghosts who might be listening. "It's just me, Joey."

After a few moments, Kerry turns to Theresa, saying, "I don't feel anything. You?"

"That's because Joey's not talking loud enough," Elbie says. "This ghost needs a good holler to get him going."

Yeah, right. If I do that, Mr. Bird will definitely freak the girls out. I ignore their questions and stare into space, trying to come up with a solution. "I've got an idea," I announce, and before anyone can stop me, I take hold of the sheet.

Like a terrified choir, Elbie, Theresa, and Kerry shout, "Nooooooooo!"

As the cloth slides across Mr. Bird's face, he sucks in a huge breath, like a drowning man coming up for air. Hands grasping, he sits up, yanking the sheet out of my hand before it gets past his chest.

All the while, the girls are screaming.

"It's okay," Elbie says, trying to calm them. "This is my dad."

Mr. Bird gapes at the crowd, his chest rising and falling heavily. Sheet clutched to his chest, he glares at Elbie who is already passing him his hearing aids. "You selling tickets now, boy?"

"No, Dad, it's not like that. We were just . . ."

"It's my fault," I tell Mr. Bird. "I thought pulling the sheet would be a good way to wake you up, but forgot you aren't wearing any pants."

Once his breathing settles down, Mr. Bird tightens the sheet around himself and looks at Kerry and Theresa. "Have we met?"

"Oh, no," Theresa says, shaking her head. "I'm Theresa Martinez, Joey's sister."

Kerry offers her hand. "And I'm Kerry Addison. Forgive our intrusion. We came down here because Elbie thought you might be able to help us."

"Help you jump out of your skin, maybe." As Mr. Bird shakes Kerry's hand, he narrows his gaze on Elbie. "Boy, I will deal with you later, but if I *ever* wake up like this again . . ."

"You won't."

"That's what you said the last time."

"Cross my heart." Elbie swipes his hand across his chest twice, then rushes to collect his dad's pants from their hanger. "Girls?" He makes a shooing motion. "Please. Can't you see my dad needs his privacy? Step out of the room for a minute."

"Of course. How inconsiderate of us." Eyes rolling, Kerry looks at Theresa who answers with her own eye roll.

Lucky for Elbie, Mr. Bird is a lot happier once he's got his pants on. He looks from me to Elbie. "I doubt if you brought those girls here just to scare them, so what's up?"

"They're helping us with a ghost thing," I say. "At school."

"Yeah," Elbie says. "You remember that librarian we buried last week, don't you Dad?"

"Of course. Sylvia Cowan. But we should probably discuss this somewhere else." He herds the four of us upstairs to his office, and once we're all seated, steps behind his desk. "So, one of my ex-clients is haunting your school library?"

"Yes," I tell him. "And I think she's holding a book I want to read hostage."

"How does a ghost hold a book hostage?"

"I think Mrs. Cowan hid it somewhere. Now, I'm worried she won't let me have it until I do something for her."

"And what is it she wants?"

"That's the problem. We don't really know."

He looks at Elbie. "What makes you think I can help, son?"

"Because we took care of her."

"Yeah, that was just a few days ago." Mr. Bird opens his laptop, and after a few clicks he's reading Mrs. Cowan's file. "Here she is. Sylvia Cowan, widow, age sixty-nine. No kids, just that jerk of a nephew." Mr. Bird draws in a deep breath and blows it out slowly. "I really shouldn't be telling you this."

"Our lips are seals," I say, hoping he'll realize how serious we all are, but instead of telling us about the dead librarian, Mr. Bird's mouth curls into a half-smile. Unsure if he believes me, I try again. "Please, Mr. Bird. If we don't help her, the library will stay closed forever."

Elbie leans forward, the palms of his hands pressed together. "Come on, Dad. They won't tell anyone."

We all shake our heads.

"And you *know* I won't," Elbie continues. "I may be a goof, but I am your son, and morticians don't blab—at least not for a very good reason."

Nodding slightly, Elbie's dad leans back in his seat, studying one face, then another. "As you might expect, I've learned a lot about ghosts in my time. And from what you've told me, this dead librarian definitely has a bone to pick with someone. Otherwise, she wouldn't be haunting that library."

I know nothing about picking bones, but I nod like everyone else.

"Promise me you won't repeat anything I tell you about this woman." Again, Mr. Bird looks at each of us. "I want to hear you say it."

We all promise.

"All right, then, here goes." Mr. Bird settles back in his chair, his gaze aimed at the framed landscape behind us. "That nephew I mentioned was a real piece of work. Always bragging about how as the only living relative, everything his aunt owned was his. And then he goes and buys the cheapest urn possible for her cremains, just one step up from a cardboard box. I'm surprised he sprung for that spot in the cemetery's new urn garden."

"What's an urn garden?" Theresa asks.

"A bunch of teeny tiny graves," Elbie says.

Mr. Bird bobs his head from side to side. "Yeah, I suppose you *could* call it that. I like to refer to them as designated areas dedicated to the interment of cremated remains."

Elbie grins. "Like I said. A bunch of teeny tiny graves. What else can you tell us, Dad?"

"Well, her funeral had no flowers whatsoever. There were no services and no obituary, online or in the paper." Mr. Bird shakes his head slowly. "That cheapskate couldn't even spare the time to bring us the clothes he wanted her to wear. I had to send your mother over so she could pick them out. The way she told it, the place was a real mess. Carpets pulled up. Holes in the walls. The guy must have been looking for the stolen money."

"What stolen money?" Elbie asks him.

"It's all rumor, really." Smiling, Mr. Bird looks at each of us. "See, my wife went to high school with one of the secretaries down at the school district offices. Around three years ago, the old lady got caught stealing the library's technology grant money. Fifteen thousand dollars' worth. Normally, that kind of story would be all over the news, but the superintendent is good friends with the police chief and she didn't want the school district's name tarnished. Together, they kept the story quiet and convinced the old lady to plead guilty in exchange for a shorter sentence."

"That's awful," Theresa says.

"Did she die in prison?" I ask.

Mr. Bird nods. "I collected the remains myself."

"But what happened to the fifteen thousand dollars?" Elbie asks.

Mr. Bird sighs. "Nobody knows. The police checked all her accounts. It wasn't in her safe deposit box. Not in her house either, and they scoured the place from top to bottom. The nephew even dug up the yard. I know because he griped about not finding anything when he came in to pay me."

"I don't understand," Kerry says. "Why would Mrs. Cowan want to hang around a place where she did something terrible?"

"Maybe she has some unfinished business there," Theresa says.

"That makes sense," I say, "but it still doesn't explain what she wants from us."

Before anyone can speak, the phone on Mr. Bird's desk rings. "Sorry, you kids are going to have to step outside—and remember, what I just told you stays between us."

"Sure, Dad. We promise." Elbie stands up and gestures for us to do the same. We thank Mr. Bird and close the office door before heading back to the lobby area.

"Well, that didn't help us much," Kerry says.

Theresa shrugs. "I thought we learned quite a bit."

"Yeah," Kerry says, "about a horrible woman who robbed a school. We still don't know what that thieving ghost woman wants Joey to do."

"Hey," Elbie says. "If we figure that out, maybe she'll tell us where she hid that money."

"I suppose it's possible. And what about all those ghosts you promised me? We've been in this mortuary a half hour and my hair hasn't stood on end once." With a crooked smile, Kerry narrows her eyes at Elbie. "I think this one lured us here just so he could play his little prank on us." She steps toward him. "I'm right, aren't I?"

"I . . . they . . ." He stumbles backward into one of his mother's big plants. "Let's go to the school."

She squints down at him. "To speak to that ghost again?"

"Why not?" Elbie says. "It's not even four o'clock yet."

"But, at this hour, the library will be locked up," I tell him. "How are we going to get in?"

Elbie sighs. "No worries. I'm tight with the most important person in the school."

"Who's that?" Kerry asks. "The secretary?"

"Oh, heck no." Elbie smiled his big Tic Tac smile. "She's the janitor."

CHAPTER 10

IT ONLY TAKES a few minutes to bike to the school. Most of the outside doors are locked at this hour, but we find one that's not and head down the main hallway. To my surprise, the lights are on in the library, and the janitor's cart is sitting outside the open door.

As we get closer, I realize Miss Beverly's vacuuming, and as I step through the doorway, I can't help but frown. Not only is my least favorite sound assaulting my ears, but I can still smell Ms. Skyeblu's sage, although it's not nearly as strong as when Elbie and I last visited. Maybe Mrs. Cowan enjoys having the place cleaned, because unlike the day she put on her little display, the temperature is comfortable now, and the lights don't even flicker. In the back of the room, wires snake out of a hole in the ceiling where a couple of those rectangular tiles have been removed.

Following the sound, we head back to the picture book section and find Miss Beverly, a short sturdy woman shaped a lot like one of those ATM machines you find in convenience stores. Her straight gray hair, the same color as her I ♥ Kentucky tee-shirt, sways back and forth as she dances the big machine along the orange carpeting.

"Look," Elbie says. "She's got headphones on."

"I wish *I* had headphones on," I grumble and clamp my hands over my ears.

He puts his mouth by my ear. "Sorry, dawg. I feel for you, but . . ." Grinning his big Tic Tac smile, he creeps toward Miss Beverly, hands outstretched and fingers waggling. Thankfully, Kerry is faster, and she jerks him back by his shirt collar before he can do any damage.

With my hands covering my ears, I can't hear what she and Theresa are telling him, but it's safe to say neither of the girls think the *Creep and Freak* is a good idea right now. Elbie seems to argue the point, but with both girls positioned between him and the still-oblivious janitor, his entire body seems to deflate. Throwing up his hands, he nods.

Zizzzzzzzzzz, zizzz, zizzzzzzzzzzzzzz.

Unaware of everything going on behind her, Miss Beverly continues to work, half vacuuming and half dancing, her long hair swaying.

"She must be listening to some pretty loud music," I say to no one in particular.

Keeping Elbie behind her, Theresa pries my hand off my right ear. "*You* get her attention, Jojo. Just be nice and remember how much you hate unexpected touches."

I nod and circle around Miss Beverly, both hands plugging my ears. Noticing me, she smiles and turns off the vacuum.

"Hey there, Joey. I see you brought some friends. What's up?"

"We came to talk to the ghost."

"What?" Miss Beverly pulls off her headphones. "What did you say?"

Elbie steps closer. "He said he lost his sweatshirt in here."

"No, I didn't."

Miss Beverly looks back and forth between the four of us. "If you kids need something, spit it out. I'm pretty much done in here, but there's still eight more rooms need vacuuming."

Elbie smiles. "Joey means he knows exactly where he left it. You can go start on another room, Miss Beverly. We'll leave as soon as we find Joey's sweatshirt."

She steps to a nearby bookshelf where a super-sized soda cup looks strangely out of place alongside a copy of *Where the Red Fern Grows*. Miss Beverly picks up the drink and takes a long suck from the straw. "Sorry, Elbie. You're a nice kid, but I trust you about as far as I can throw you. Y'all have a look, but I'm staying put."

"Oooh-kaaaay." Sounding and acting a lot like Eeyore, Elbie herds us toward the non-fiction section on the opposite side of the room. "Come on, guys. Let's go find that sweatshirt."

"But I didn't lose my sweatshirt," I whisper to Theresa.

"Shhh." She takes my elbow and hustles me through the now normal looking library as Miss Beverly watches. When we get to the animal books, she stops and turns to Elbie. "I guess she doesn't think she can throw you very far." Her mouth turns down. "Now what do we do?"

Frowning, Elbie looks at the carpet.

"Yes, what?" Kerry says, also frowning. "We can't very well speak to the ghost with that woman watching our every move."

As I've seen other people do when they're frustrated, I throw up my arms. "Then, I guess we go home."

Theresa's eyes wander to a small wall niche where the books on foreign countries are kept. "No, wait." She steps over to the wall. Above the books hang seven wooden plaques, all of which are hanging at strange angles.

"I never noticed those before," I say as we all walk over. "Have you, Elbie?"

"Nope. Guess that's because neither of us looks for books in this area."

Their brass plates are tarnished and nearly impossible to read. Squinting hard, I straighten one and read the words out loud. "Sylvia Cowan, Librarian of the Year, Fern Creek School District."

"So, she got an award," Elbie says. "Probably been there for years."

"These other plaques are hers too," Theresa tells him. "She won them. Seven times in twenty years. Mrs. Cowan loved her job, *and* she loved this library."

"She didn't take the grant money," I whisper.

Theresa nods. "You don't steal from something you love."

"But she must have," Kerry says. "She pled guilty."

"Sure," Elbie whispers, "but that stuff happens on TV all the time. Lawyers talk their clients into it. You know, so they'll get a lighter sentence."

From back in the main area, Miss Beverly calls out, asking how we're doing. Kerry says she sounds impatient, so we send Elbie back to beg for more time.

"Okay," Theresa says, "so there's a good chance Mrs. Cowan really isn't a crook. That still doesn't get us any closer to talking to her."

While the others argue over what to do next, I spot a broken piece of pencil lying on a nearby shelf and sigh. If I take it, we can get back into the library without Miss Beverly's help or even her knowing. But should I? I pull Theresa aside and fill her in.

"That's perfect, Jojo. You have to do it."

"I want that book, but breaking into the library is wrong."

At first, Theresa looks like she's suddenly developed a stomachache. But she notices Miss Beverly watching us, and her lips form a smile.

"Look," she whispers. "This is another one of those iffy situations like the time Kerry and I snuck into the attic. Yes, Dad told me not to go up there, but if we didn't, I never would have met my twin sister's ghost or learned how she died."

"I remember," I whisper, studying my sneakers as if expecting to find the perfect solution scrawled across them.

"Okay, so we don't have permission to come in here. But you know what will happen if we don't help Mrs. Cowan. And that's a lot more important than any old bug book."

"Yeah. Her spirit will never rest if we don't prove who really took that grant money."

"Exactly. Can you deal with that? For me, not helping that poor lady is a lot bigger crime than what we're planning to do."

Ugh. I hate iffy situations. Realizing there's logic in Theresa's words, I wave Kerry and Elbie back toward the exit. "Come on, guys. Let's go. Sorry to waste your time, Miss Beverly. I guess my sweatshirt wasn't in the library after all." With the broken pencil in my pocket and a knot in my stomach, I march outside and watch as the others shuffle after me, the janitor bringing up the rear.

Miss Beverly rolls her vacuum cleaner out into the hallway, then turns off all the lights and, once she tugs the door shut, turns to me and says, "You should check the lost and found tomorrow."

I search for an answer that isn't a lie, then settle for, "I didn't think of that."

Satisfied the library is locked tight, Miss Beverly says her goodbyes and pushes her cart to the next classroom.

"Now what?" Elbie asks, once we turn the corner at the end of the hallway. He and Kerry stare as I press my back to the wall and slide down into a crouch. "We hide here until she goes into the next classroom."

"What good is that?" Kerry says. "The library is still locked."

"Just wait," Theresa tells her.

Grumbling, Elbie posts himself as our lookout.

"She's parking her cart in front of B-7," he tells us. "Now she's coming back for the vacuum." He giggles. "Now she's scratching her butt."

"Way too much information," Kerry says.

"Just tell us when she's inside B-7," I tell Elbie.

After a few seconds, he announces that she has. I signal for them to follow, and the four of us tiptoe back to the library door.

"Now what?" Elbie glances over his shoulder at B-7's open door where Miss Beverly's vacuum cleaner is now back at work.

"Now, we go back inside." I rest my hand on the knob. Theresa is right. Yes, we're going in without permission, and yes, we'll definitely get in big trouble if we're caught. But it's not like we plan on stealing anything. We're doing this for Mrs. Cowan, at least mostly. Satisfied I'm doing the right thing, I pull hard, and as I expect, the door springs open with a sticky pop.

"Whoa!" Elbie looks me up and down. "Who'd you learn that trick from, Harry Houdini?"

"No, from Kyle Hammett." I point out the broken pencil I dropped at the foot of the door, now squashed against the sill. "It kept the lock from shutting all the way. Back at my old school, Kyle used this method to sneak into the classroom and steal the teachers' reward candy." I pick up the slightly flattened pencil and shoo them inside. "Kyle got caught, so let's hurry up and get inside."

The four of us hustle into the dark library, and Elbie grabs the flashlights from Ms. Skyeblu's desk just as a soft thud turns our heads toward the little kid section.

"Sounds like another book falling," he whispers. "Wait here." Elbie trots off, the light of his flashlight bouncing. It isn't long before he's back, a large picture book clasped between his fingers. He holds it up, and Kerry shines the other flashlight on it.

The Thank You Book.

"I think Mrs. Cowan is thanking us for figuring out she's not a thief," Kerry says.

"Well, she's welcome." Theresa rubs her arms. "You guys feel that? I think she's close."

It's true. It is colder, and the little hairs on the back of my neck have started to prickle. If Mrs. Cowan was on the other side of the room before, she's practically on top of us now.

Kerry grins. "God, I love this stuff." She throws one arm around an already rigid-looking Theresa, making her squeak. "Come on, let's see if she'll appear for us."

"She can't," Elbie says.

"Why not?"

"My dad says, once a body's been cremated, they can't manifest anymore."

"Oh?" Kerry seems to mull over the information, then blows out her cheeks. "That's all right. There's more than one way to communicate." Before anyone can comment, Kerry places her flashlight on a nearby table and looks at the ceiling. "Hello, Mrs. Cowan. You already know Joey and Elbie. My name is Kerry, and this is Joey's sister, Theresa." She takes Theresa's hand and tries to lift it, but Theresa snatches it away. "Sorry," Kerry tells the ghost. "She's actually very nice. Just a little uncomfortable around spirits."

"That's not true." Theresa crosses her arms. "Just the ones I don't know."

"Point taken," Kerry tells her.

Since Elbie's shining the second light up at the ceiling, that's where Kerry focuses her gaze when she addresses Mrs. Cowan again. "We learned what happened to you from Elbie's dad, the mortician who cremated your body. We'd like to help, if we can. Do you mind answering a few questions?"

Everyone stares at the flashlight on the table, but nothing happens.

"Maybe you should explain what she's supposed to do with it," I suggest. "You know, the rules."

"Blimey, you're right. I'm such a twit." Kerry shifts from one foot to the other. "Sorry, Mrs. Cowan. We've seen this done on TV, but it's the first time we've actually tried it ourselves. If you don't mind, we're going to ask you a few questions. If the answer is yes, click the flashlight on like this." She slides the button to the on position. "If the answer is no, then don't do anything." Kerry switches the flashlight off. "Do you understand what I've been saying to you?"

The light clicks on.

"Brilliant," Kerry says. "Joey, what would you like to ask Mrs. Cowan?"

"I want to know why she's holding my bug book hostage."

Everyone looks at the flashlight.

"The light's already on," Elbie says. "Plus, we can only ask yes or no questions."

Muttering to herself, Kerry snaps the light off. "There. Now, go ahead, Jojo. Ask."

With a better understanding of how the game works, I reformulate my question and say, "Can I please have *Poisonous Spiders of the World?*"

Instead of turning the flashlight on, a book skids across the table, making all of us jump.

"What the heck?" Elbie shines the other flashlight on it, eyes wide because of his surprise. "It's that *Hostage* book again."

Already starting to wheeze, Kerry draws in a deep, slightly squeaky breath, and blows it out slowly. "Soooo, you really are holding the book hostage?" Eyes glued to the flashlight, she pulls her asthma inhaler out from her pocket.

When the light clicks on, she grins.

Elbie snaps off the flashlight. "Is that because you want us to do something for you?"

Yes.

"What were the names of those other books?" Kerry asks me.

"*Betrayed* and *Stolen Treasure.*"

"*Stolen Treasure?*" Theresa gasps. "That must be the grant money they say she stole. What if—" Before she can finish, another book flies by, fanning Theresa's hair. She spins around, then back again. "What was that?"

"Another book, duh." Elbie picks it up and shines the light on its cover. "Ha! It's *Liar, Liar* by Gary Paulsen." He chuckles. "Good one, Mrs. Cowan. So, you're saying you *didn't* steal that money?"

Yes.

I turn the flashlight off. "We didn't think so, but if *you* didn't steal the money, then who did?"

Nothing happens.

"Yes or no questions," Kerry says. "The other book title was *Betrayed*. Were you betrayed by someone, Mrs. Cowan?"

Yes.

"Was it your nephew? The one who inherited your house?"

Nothing happens.

"That's a no," Elbie says. "Was it the new librarian trying to get your job?"

Nothing happens.

Kerry chuffs. "At this rate, we'll be here all night."

"We have to do it methodically," I tell them. "Like a game of twenty questions."

"Was it someone else?" Theresa asks.

"Obviously," I tell her.

Theresa's mouth twists to the side. "Now I remember why I never liked this game."

I try again. "Is it someone who works here at school?"

Yes.

Elbie pumps his fist. "I knew it."

"A student or a teacher?" Theresa asks.

"How can she possibly answer that?" Kerry says. "One question at a time."

"Okay, okay. Was it a student?"

No.

"Was it a teacher?"

No.

"Well, if it wasn't a student, and it wasn't a teacher, who does that leave?" Theresa asks.

"Lots of people." Elbie counts them off on his fingers. "There's the janitor, the secretaries, the yard duties . . ."

"This is taking too long," Kerry says. "Isn't there a faster way to eliminate some of them? We have to get out of here before someone catches us."

"Male or female," I tell them. "That would get rid of a lot."

"Good idea," Elbie says. "Were you betrayed by a man, Mrs. Cowan?"

Yes.

Elbie and I bump knuckles. "That cuts out a lot of people," he says. "All that's left are the night janitor, that old yard duty guy, and . . ."

Kerry holds both hands out in front of her as if asking Elbie to stop talking. "Okay, I've got this. Mrs. Cowan? The boys are going to list all of male employees. Turn the flashlight on when one of them mentions the person who betrayed you. Make sense?"

The light turns on.

"Good." Kerry clicks it back off. "Joey, you start."

"Was it the old yard duty guy?"

Nothing.

"The night janitor, Mr. Andres?"

Nothing.

"I have one," Elbie says. "How about that old crossing guard, Mr. Bob?"

Nothing.

We all look at each other and shrug.

"Who have you left out?" Kerry asks.

Elbie bangs his hand on the table. "The principal."

Immediately, the light flashes, *yes, yes, yes.*

"Finally!" I bang my hand too. "You hit the snail right on the head."

"I *knew* there was something dirty about that guy," Elbie says. "And that's nail, not snail."

I blow out a sigh. "Okay, but how is Mr. Nguyen dirty? He's always wearing suits, and I've never even seen one smudge on his—"

"Dawg, I wasn't talking about his hygiene, I meant—"

"Enough of this." Kerry waves her hand in our faces. "Now, let me get this straight, Mrs. Cowan. You're telling us that Principal Nguyen is a big liar who stole fifteen thousand dollars' worth of grant money and you went to jail for it?"

Again, the flashlight goes crazy.

"How can we possibly prove that?" Theresa says.

From out of the darkness a book comes skidding across the carpet, landing at Elbie's feet. He picks it up. "It's called *Report to the Principal's Office*, by Jerry Spinelli. Funny book." Elbie looks at me. "You think she wants us to check out Mr. Nguyen's office?"

The flashlight blinks.

"Easy to say," Theresa says. "But how? You sure can't say you left your sweatshirt in *there*."

Elbie puffs his chest out. "That's easy. I've been sent to the office lots of times. All I have to do is . . ." Suddenly, his face looks like all the happy has been washed off of it. "Dang it, I almost forgot. My folks said that if Mr. Nguyen calls them again they're going to take away my video games for a year." He turns to me, one eyebrow raised. "How about you, Jojo? You've never even been there."

"No way." Theresa throws up her hands. "They'll call the house. The last thing we need is to involve our dad in this."

Grinning, Elbie nudges me. "But Mr. Nguyen doesn't call parents if it's your first time. Remember the second day of school, Joey? That Mickey kid started pushing you around at recess, so when we got back into the classroom I poured water on his seat and he sat down on it."

I nod. "He looked like he wet his pants."

"Yeah, it was great. Everybody laughed. Then, Mr. Minelli sent me to the office, but since I was new here, all Mr. Nguyen did was lecture me and assign me one recess detention."

"Perfect," Kerry says. "Are you all right with a lecture and detention, Joey?"

"I think so." But that means I have to break some kind of rule.

"Okay, Mrs. Cowan," Kerry says. "It looks like Joey's going to check out Mr. Nguyen's office for you. We'll come back later when we know more."

"I'm tired of sneaking around. Let's go home." Theresa starts for the door, but Elbie stops her.

"Wait," he whispers. "What if somebody's out there?"

He tiptoes over to the main entrance and peers through the narrow window slit. "From what I can see there's nobody in the main hallway. Hang on." Slowly, Elbie turns the knob and pushes the door open just enough to peer down the hall. "Everybody hide. It's Miss Beverly again *and* Mr. Nguyen." He shuts the door and dives behind the closest bookcase.

Theresa grabs my hand and pulls me behind the shelf where Kerry and Elbie are already crouching.

I find a gap between some books and peer through just as keys rattle outside. The sound is quickly followed by the door swinging open. Miss Beverly stomps in and flips on all the lights. "See? Look at that mess they left me."

Mr. Nguyen rolls his eyes. I'm not sure what that means. Maybe he doesn't like Miss Beverly. He follows the janitor across the library to the gaping hole in the ceiling where wires dangle like giant spider legs.

"I don't get it," he says. "What's the big deal? Obviously, they're still working on it."

"Seriously?" Miss Beverly throws up her arms. "Look at all the little doodads they left on my rug. I can't vacuum that up." She steps forward, finger pointing. "See? Plastic." She takes another step. "Wire . . . screw . . . wire, wire, wire—I'd have to crawl around on my hands and knees to get it all up."

"Oh, geez, fine. I'll phone Bob Jenkins as soon as I get back to my office. Anything else?"

"Yeah, tell him to remind Gustavo and Tony that I'm not their maid and to stop treating me like I am."

"Oh, sure. Like that's going to help." Mr. Nguyen tips his head toward the door. "Okay, so I saw the big mess. Anything else? You're not the only one around here with things to do."

"Yeah, I just remembered I left my drink cup in here. You see it?"

"Oh, my God, woman, are you still drinking soda?"

"Yeah, yeah, I know, sugar's bad. I thought I left it here . . ." She pats the shelf beside her. "But I also remember sipping on it when I was dusting those blue shelves over there."

We all duck down as their heads turn our way. Blue shelves? *We're* behind the blue shelves. Is she coming toward us? Is Mr. Nguyen? Afraid they'll see me, I don't peek. What do we do? Hunch our way to the other side of the library? No, they'd hear us for sure. I squeeze my eyes shut and pray for Miss Beverly to hurry up and find what she's looking for. When I open them, Theresa's eyes are wide. So are Kerry's and Elbie's. Are they as scared as I am?

"Hey, look," Mr. Nguyen says. "Isn't that it over on the check-out desk?"

Miss Beverly chuckles. "Oh, yeah. How about that. We walked right past it."

I gather my courage and peer out between the books. To my relief, she's sipping her soda and already heading for the door.

"Could have sworn I left it back there." Again, she points in our direction, and again, we all duck down.

Maybe Mrs. Cowan moved it. If she can throw a book . . .

"You shouldn't be drinking that stuff anyway," Mr. Nguyen says. "You should make your own vegetable smoothies, like me."

"Yeah, yeah."

They turn off the lights and lock the door behind them.

"That was close," Elbie says.

We stand up and look at the door.

"I'm tired of this," I whisper. "I want to go home."

"Stay here." Elbie creeps back to the door and peeks through the window slit again. "Dang it! They're still out there." After pressing his ear to the door for a few seconds, he slips back behind the bookcase to where the rest of us are waiting.

"What are they doing?" Theresa asks.

"One of the kindergarten teachers just walked up. She's freaking out about her new alphabet rug. Some kid threw up on O for octopus today. Miss Beverly thinks they shouldn't even have carpeting, but Mr. Nguyen says—"

"Oh-my-god." Theresa pounds her fists against her thighs. "Doesn't this place have another door?"

"Yeah, back there," Elbie says. "But if we open it, an alarm will go off."

"How long are they going to talk?" Theresa asks.

Kerry pulls out her cell phone.

"I didn't think that was possible," I tell her.

"What?"

"Searching the Internet for how long they're going to talk."

"That's not what I'm doing." After some taps to the screen she scrolls down, then smiles and taps the screen one more time. "Watch this." She holds the phone to her ear.

"Who are you calling?" Theresa asks.

"The school. I'll tell them I'm Miss Beverly's niece and ask them to call her down to the office."

"In your British accent?" Theresa snatches the phone from Kerry and presses it to her own ear. "Well, howdy. I'm looking for my Aunt Beverly."

"Is that supposed to be a southern accent?" Elbie's face puckers.

"That's right," Theresa says into the phone. "She's the day janitor. I'm callin' from down south. We got ourselves a family e-mergency. Can you git her for me right quick? Great. Thank yeeeew." Theresa grins and covers the phone with her hand. "Elbie, go watch."

He runs over to the door. After a minute or so, he waves us over.

"They just called Miss Beverly on her walky-talky," Elbie tells us. "She ran down to the office. The others are gone too. I'm going to stick my head out now. If the hall's empty, we're out of here. Okay?" He opens the door again and first pushes his face into the crack. "So far so good." He pokes his head out. "Let's go. Miss Beverly's not going to stay down there very long."

We move out into the hallway, and as we speed walk to the nearest exit, a tiny hello makes us jump. It's Miss Beverly, answering Kerry's phone call.

Without stopping, Theresa puts Kerry's phone to her ear and says, "What's up? Huh? No I didn't. Please don't call this number again." She disconnects and hands the phone back to Kerry, who holds open the door so we can finally leave the building.

As we ride our bikes home from our little library adventure, Elbie never runs out of suggestions for how I can get myself sent to the principal's office. With the four of us riding side by side along the quiet neighborhood streets, he starts by offering to loan me a whoopy cushion so I can slide it under Mr. Minelli just before he sits down. I don't like that, so he suggests I go to the bathroom and throw some wet toilet paper balls up on the ceiling.

"But who's going to catch me?" I ask. "There aren't any teachers in the bathroom."

"Just sing while you're doing it. Someone will hear you."

"No thanks. The janitors already have enough work. I don't want to give them more."

"Okay, then how about when someone starts to sit down, you pull the chair out from under them? That's a classic."

Since I'm terrible at multitasking, I wonder how Elbie can think up so many different ideas without falling off his bike. "What if they get hurt?" I ask him.

"They won't get hurt."

"How do you know?"

"I just do."

"Think of something else," Kerry says.

"Okay," Elbie says. "How about starting a food fight?"

"Nothing too messy," I tell him.

"Okay, how about this? When someone's carrying their lunch tray through the cafeteria, you stick out your leg and trip them."

"No way," Theresa says. "That's messy *and* dangerous."

He slaps his forehead. "I'm giving you my best stuff here."

"Sorry, but Kerry and Theresa are right. Plus, I don't feel comfortable doing any of those things. Let me think about it tonight. I'll have something by tomorrow. I promise."

CHAPTER 11

IT TAKES ME a while to settle on the perfect way to get myself in trouble, but the next morning I'm ready for action. Elbie won't stop nagging, but I refuse to share my plan. He pesters me with questions the entire bike ride to school. Is it this? Is it that? I shake my head every time.

"If I tell you, it won't work," I say as we join the line of kids outside Mr. Minelli's room. "Don't you want it to work?"

"Yes, but—"

"Then stop asking me questions. You'll know soon enough."

About a half hour before morning recess I head to the pencil sharpener, which is near the open classroom door. Once nobody's looking, I break off a piece of pencil and stuff it against the doorjamb with my shoe. Satisfied it's in place, I return to my seat.

Not long after, the bell rings for recess. Instead of running out to play, I tell Elbie I need to use the bathroom and promise I'll meet him by the tetherball poles in a few minutes. Knowing Mr. Minelli has recess duty, I use my broken pencil trick to sneak into the locked classroom. I feel weird being in there with so many empty desks, as if aliens have abducted everyone but me. It doesn't take long to set things up.

I head out to the playground, and after a few very competitive games of tetherball with Elbie, the bell rings and we head back to class. Exhausted, we flop into our seats. The teacher has Elbie sitting in the front row with me behind him. On Elbie's desk are a few sheets of paper, a pencil, and a plastic water bottle filled to the brim.

"Hot out there today," I say, wiping my forehead with the back of my arm. I pick up my own water bottle and take a long swig.

Seeing me drink, Elbie picks up his own bottle and unscrews the top. But before it reaches his lips, water spurts from several tiny holes at the bottom of the bottle. It not only wets the papers on his desk, but his tee-shirt and cargo shorts too.

"Hey!" Elbie shouts. As the class erupts with laughter, he races to the sink, holding the sprinkler-bottle at arm's length.

"Elbie!" Mr. Minelli barks. Thin lips pressed into a scowl, he storms over and glares down at the trail of wet carpeting. "I thought we had an agreement."

"We do." Elbie frowns down at his clothes. The damp spot on his shorts looks a lot like a pee stain. He groans and grabs a handful of paper towels.

"You shoulda went to the bathroom at recess!" a red-headed boy named Andrew shouts.

Again, the classroom sounds like a monkey cage. I cover my ears. At first, I think they're laughing at Andrew's bad grammar. Then I notice a lot of the kids are pointing at Elbie. Scowling, he grabs another handful of paper towels and dabs at the wet spot.

Since Elbie has pranked me almost every day since school started, I expected to enjoy this more. But I don't. In fact, I feel terrible. From the look on his face, it's even obvious to me that Elbie isn't having any fun. Hoping he'll learn something from this, I let him suffer a few moments longer, but when the teacher starts writing Elbie a referral, I speak up.

"It's not his fault," I tell Mr. Minelli as I trot over to his big wooden desk, but he shakes his head.

"You're a good friend, Joey. But it's wrong for you to cover for him." The referral form consists of three small papers, white, pink, and yellow, glued together at the top.

Mr. Minelli fills it out and tears off the top copy. The rest, he holds out to Elbie.

I take it instead, and all talking stops. It's so quiet I can hear is the aquarium bubbling, and that's on the opposite side of the room.

"What are you doing?" Mr. Minelli asks me.

"Elbie didn't make those holes in the water bottle. I did."

After a class-wide gasp there's a sudden burst of chatter, but I don't bother listening. Instead, I focus on Elbie.

Still holding the same handful of paper towels, he stands there, mouth opening and closing, a lot like Bubbles, our class fish. I consider telling him that, but decide he probably doesn't want to hear it right now.

"*You* did this?" Elbie's gaze drops to his pants, then back up to me.

"Yeah. It was my first prank. Funny, huh?"

He gives the front of his shorts another dab. "Yeah . . . good one."

I pass the referral back to Mr. Minelli, whose eyes are even wider than everyone else's. "If it's okay, you can scratch out Elbie's name and write mine in above," I tell him. "There's no sense in wasting a good referral form."

AS I MAKE my way down the main hallway, the smell of hot grease floats my way, telling me the cooks are getting ready for lunch. The library door is propped open too. Nothing strange there. What's unusual is the sound of Ms. Skyeblu screaming.

Ready to cup my hands over my ears if she continues, I peer inside just as the freaked-out librarian comes storming out, the fringe on her suede jacket sleeves flapping. Since the touch of anything leather annoys me, I Immediately back up, putting space between us.

"That's it!" she shouts. "Out of my way, Joey, I'm going home!"

Aware that people often yell because they're upset about something, I ask what happened as she slams the library door shut behind her.

"There's something freaky going on in there," Ms. Skyeblu mutters as she struggles to fit the key into the lock. "And it's got nothing to do with the doggone electrical system." She leans toward me, her wide buggy eyes inches from mine. "Bad mojo, man. Bad mojo."

The word bad, I understand. Mojo, not so much. Still worried I might come in contact with all that flapping leather, I take two more steps back and tell her I'm sorry, an expression that seems to work in most situations.

It must help, because for a quick moment, a tiny smile touches her lips. Am I expected to smile back? As I weigh my choices, she rushes toward me saying, "If you're headed to the office, tell Miss Juanita I'm going home." Before I can get out of her way, she brushes past me, and I shudder as the leather fringe sweeps across my arm.

"Okay." I rub the feeling of dead cow off my arm and continue walking down the empty hallway.

ON THE WALL opposite the office hang six framed photos. Three women. Three men. All past principals, except for the one on the far right, which is Mr. Nguyen's. In it, he's leaning against his desk, arms crossed and a faint smile on his lips. Was he nervous when they took the picture? Defensive? Not likely, from my experiences with him. I step inside and slide the referral slip over the counter to the secretary as I repeat what Ms. Skyeblu told me to say.

Miss Juanita, a friendly lady with a helmet of tight blond curls, listens silently, her hot pink lips slightly open. After a few moments she thanks me and tells me to take a spot on the empty wooden bench behind me. After blinking down at my referral a few times, she gets up and slips through a doorway on the back wall. Getting more anxious by the minute, I focus on the smell of coffee and donuts, which is coming from the room she just came from. A few moments later, Miss Juanita is back, carrying more of the donut smell with her.

"Mr. Nguyen will see you now, Joey."

I stand up and shuffle behind the counter then walk toward the back wall and the dim donut-smelling doorway. There's a strange feeling in my chest, tight, as if I expect someone's going to jump out and scare me. I remember Elbie saying this was the easy part and immediately feel like punching him. How could he think this is easy? Then I remember the look on his face as he raced to the sink carrying that spurting water bottle.

Since I've never been in trouble for anything, I'm not sure where I'm going. What I do know is that the coffee and donut smell is getting stronger. And it's no wonder. Just inside the doorway is a small kitchen and a pink half-open box of pastries. A room on the opposite side of the hall is lined with filing cabinets. At the end are two doors. One is open. Spotting a sink and toilet, I knock on the other one.

A man's voice invites me to come in, so I turn the knob and push. The scents of cologne and coffee rise up to greet me. Mr. Nguyen is sitting behind a big wooden desk with his suitcoat hanging on the back of his chair. There's an open laptop to his left and a lime-green notepad to his right. Alongside it is a cup of coffee. For some reason, I expect Mr. Nguyen to look different, now that I know he's a criminal. But he doesn't. Shirtsleeves rolled up to his elbows, Mr. Nguyen smooths his dark hair with both hands before motioning for me to sit down. Since the chair is made of leather, I try not to touch it with my hands, thankful I decided to wear long pants today.

Hands clasped tightly in front of me, I focus on my breathing and stare at the wall clock to my right. In the center is a horse and jockey. Since the hour hand points to the horse's head and the minute hand to its back, I decide that makes the time ten-fifteen. Realizing I probably don't have a lot of time, I check the room for clues while the principal reads what Mr. Minelli wrote.

Having never been in a principal's office before, I can only compare it to the other offices I've been in. That's pretty much just my doctor's and Elbie's Dad's. The furniture here is similar: a desk with one chair on one side and two on the other. But unlike the mortuary office, which is mostly beige with one dull landscape, the artwork here is tons more colorful and there's a lot more of it. Some of it is kid stuff, watercolor rainbows and construction paper mosaics. But the majority of the pictures are framed, and those are the ones with horses in them. Specifically, racehorses.

Mr. Nguyen's chair creaks, and I glance back at him. Instead of my referral form, he's looking at his computer screen, which, from this angle, I can barely see.

Noticing my gaze, he says, "Mind your manners please," and tips the monitor toward himself, cutting off what little view I have.

After about a minute, he picks up the referral form and reads it.

"This behavior is not like you, is it, Joey?"

"No, sir." I consider asking him if stealing grant money and blaming it on others is like him, but I don't. Heart beating its way through my ribcage, I notice a smudge of dirt on one of my fingers and almost rub it off on the chair cushion before I remember I'm sitting on dead cow.

Time passes slowly. I sit. I look around. Is this a form of kid torture? Elbie would definitely think so. The clock's minute hand points to the horse's butt, ten-twenty, and Mr. Nguyen still isn't saying anything. I glance over to find him studying the computer screen again. After a few moments, he writes down a few notes on the lime-green pad.

His preoccupation with the computer does have one positive aspect. It gives me more time to complete my mission. I look around the room, but with so much stuff on the walls, I have a hard time knowing what's a clue and what isn't. There's a chalk drawing of a lion's face over to my left. Is that what I'm looking for, and how am I supposed to know?

"Why did you do it?" Mr. Nguyen says.

Startled, I look up, expecting to make eye contact, but from what I can tell, that's not going to be a problem. Mr. Nguyen is writing more stuff on his notepad. I continue my search for clues as I give him the answer I prepared last night and say, "Because Elbie always plays pranks on me."

"I see."

Seeing his's attention drift back to the computer, I scan a patch of horseracing pictures, pausing at one in which the jockey is wearing pink and green silks, a lot like Mr. Prendergast's. I wonder where he is now.

Two minutes later, Mr. Nguyen seems to have forgotten me for whatever is on the computer screen. What am I looking for? I might as well be blind. Realizing what a lousy detective I am, I suddenly want to fast-forward through this whole ordeal. But I can't. I'm stuck here until this man—no, this criminal—remembers that I'm still here and finishes up with me.

Five more minutes pass, with the clock's minute hand now pointing to the horse's back knee. By now, I know all the kids' names on all the kid art and most of the horses' names too. Not sure what to do, I look past Mr. Nguyen at the short forest-green curtains covering the short but wide window high on the wall behind him. Closed against the bright morning sun, their edges glow. Below the window hangs another framed photograph. Like most of the other pictures, it's of a big brown horse. I read the tiny metal plaque at the bottom for the third time. Secretariat. If I ever own a horse, I'm sure not naming it that.

" . . . can you tell me?"

Is he talking to me? "I'm sorry, what?" I tear my attention away from the racing photos to find Mr. Nguyen staring across the desk at me. Again, I shift my gaze to the wall clock.

"I asked what it means to you," Mr. Nguyen says.

"What *what* means to me?"

"The expression, an eye for an eye. What does it mean to you?"

Elbie never said anything about a test. Did people collect eyeballs at one time? Since my old teacher told me to answer a question with another question when I don't understand, I say, "Is that a bartering system, like from back before people used money?"

Instead of answering, he stares at me with one dark eyebrow raised, his head turned slightly to the side. Even though I'm better at reading facial expressions than I was last year, I still can't figure out what he's thinking. After several long seconds of watching me study his necktie, he leans back in his chair and flips the page on his notepad. "Are you messing with me?"

Obviously, bartering isn't the answer he was looking for. "I don't understand."

"Okay, forget I asked." He glances at the computer and scribbles down some more words before turning back to me. "Did you enjoy pranking Elbie?"

"No."

"Why not?"

I shift my gaze to a different horse picture. "Because everyone was laughing at him. He looked sad."

"And?"

"I prefer it when he smiles." Wishing Mr. Nguyen's focus was back on his computer screen, I shift in my seat to look at the black and white photographs on the wall to my right. One has a lot of horses in it. They're running hard, and the jockeys all have their butts in the air.

"Joey, do you plan on pranking anyone else?"

"No sir. Like I said, I didn't enjoy it."

"Good."

A zipping sound makes me look back, and I see Mr. Nguyen has torn the top sheet off his spiral notebook. He wads it up and tosses it into a round wastebasket, which, like most everything in the office, has racehorses on it.

"But there still has to be a consequence," Mr. Nguyen says, already starting another list. "At lunchtime, you will report to the head playground supervisor, Mrs. Randall. She'll assign you a seat at the detention table."

My chest tightens at the sudden change of routine. Normally, I sit with Elbie at the table assigned to Mr. Minelli's class. The detention table is on the opposite side of the cafeteria. I think back to Elbie and the way every kid in the class was laughing and pointing at him. "Give me two detentions."

"Feeling a little guilty, huh?" He stands up and his eyes flick back at the computer for just a second before walking me to the door. "You're a good kid, Joey. You could be a good role model for Elbie."

I thank him and give his office one more look. What am I going to tell the others, that the man likes horses? Heck, Elbie already knows that. He's been here a dozen times. Ugh, I hate spying. As Elbie would say, it's definitely not my thing.

Mr. Nguyen opens the door and stands there, waiting for me to leave.

Unable to come up with anything better, I ask, "What's with all the horse pictures?" My phrasing comes out like Elbie's.

Mr. Nguyen grins, a little disturbing since I've never seen him smile before. "Ah, I thought you seemed interested. That one's Seattle Slew," he says, pointing. "And there's War Admiral and Secretariat. All Triple Crown winners. Beautiful creatures, aren't they?"

Wondering what a triple crown would look like, I nod and fumble for something else to say. "They look fast," is all I can manage, but it's enough to keep the man talking.

"Oh, yeah, super-fast. Have you ever seen a horserace, Joey?"

I think back. "I don't know. On TV, maybe."

"Oh, there's nothing like a live race. Standing at the rail as the horses gallop past, hooves thundering, dirt flying." He sticks his chest out. "I'm going to the Kentucky Derby next May, if I can get time off."

"Nice." Not sure what more I can say, I wave goodbye and close the door behind me, doubting my visit was worth one lunch detention and definitely not two.

CHAPTER 12

I GET BACK to class expecting Elbie to ask me what happened during my visit with Mr. Nguyen. But he doesn't. In fact, he won't even look at me. Lunchtime comes, but he ditches me by running to the front of the food line. Since I have to eat at the detention table, we don't speak the rest of the afternoon. He even runs off without me at the end of the day.

Ever since I realized Elbie was upset about the prank I played on him I've had this uncomfortable feeling in my chest. I can't say it's pain, exactly, but something dark is definitely growing inside me. Is that guilt? What if Elbie never forgives me? I sling my backpack over my shoulder and trudge outside, expecting to ride home alone. But when I turn the corner near the bike racks, I stop in my tracks. Elbie's still here.

"Are you mad at me?" I ask.

"Shouldn't I be? You embarrassed me in front of everyone." He crosses his arms, a gesture I've learned can mean a lot of things.

"I'm sorry Elbie. I thought you'd appreciate the joke."

To my surprise, a huge grin spreads across his face, and he beams his big Tic Tac smile at me. "Ha ha! Got you back."

"You're not mad?"

"I was . . . until I realized why you did it."

The dark thing in my chest begins to shrivel, and I slump against the shaded cafeteria wall, suddenly lighter. "You had me worried," I say, realizing I'm smiling.

"Well, don't. I've only known you for a month and a half, and how many times have I pranked you?"

I think back. "I don't know . . . ten?"

Forehead misty with sweat, he moves into the shade beside me. "More like twice that, so how could I possibly be mad over a little payback? Come on, give me some, down low." He holds his hand out for me to slap but pulls it back and giggles as I fan the air. "Uh oh. Too slow. But seriously, Joey, I'm proud of you. That was amazing."

Since people sometime shrug when they're unsure how to respond, that's what I do.

"Okay, spill it, man. Tell me what you learned."

I tell Elbie everything I remember from my visit to the office: how Mr. Nguyen has three watercolor rainbows and two construction paper mosaics tacked to his wall. How he plans on going to the Kentucky Derby in May. I even described how his shirt sleeves were rolled up.

"Well that doesn't help us. Don't you remember anything else? Any suspicious behavior?"

"Like what?"

"I don't know. Think."

"Okay, I'll try." I lean against the wall and close my eyes. "First, I sat down in the chair . . . he asked me questions . . . I looked at the pictures on the wall . . . he looked at his computer. In fact, the whole time I was there, he kept looking at his computer screen."

That must be what Elbie wants to hear, because I open my eyes and find him hopping from one foot to the other. "That's what I'm talking about," he says, still hopping. "Now what was on the screen?"

"I don't know. It was facing him, not me."

"Dang it! Can't any of this come easy?" As he thinks, his hands flutter like two crazy butterflies, then suddenly they fly up, grab my shirt, and press me to the wall. "I got it!"

Surprised, I swipe at his hands. "Hey, get off me."

"Sorry, sorry." He springs back. "I just figured out how we can get a peek at Mr. Nguyen's computer screen."

"El-beeee! I promised him I wouldn't get into any more trouble."

"You won't," he tells me. "Now, come on, I'll show you what I'm talking about."

Wishing I shared his confidence, I follow him around the building to the kindergarten side of the school. At this hour, the miniature playground is empty. No kids, no parents, just us, the jungle gym, and a stray red ball being slowly pushed across the blacktop by the breeze. Three windows run side by side along the tall brick wall beside us, none of which I can see into because they're all six feet above the pavement.

"What are we doing here?" I ask him.

Elbie tips his head back and peers up at the far right window. "That's Mr. Nguyen's office."

I look back at the window, then at him. "And how do you know that?"

He shakes his head slowly. "Son, you're looking, but you're not seeing."

What does that even mean? I peer up at the window, which is about two feet high and four feet wide. The curtains are open and the lights are off inside, but from this angle, all I can see is the ceiling . . . *and* a small stained-glass light catcher shaped like a running horse.

"How long has that been hanging there?"

"Since forever. He keeps the curtains shut in the morning when the sun hits. Same time you were in there." He drops his backpack on the sidewalk, takes mine, and sets it beside his. Now, come on, let's do this." He laces his fingers together and holds the little saddle out in front of him. "Go ahead. Climb on."

"And do what?"

He looks up. "And look through the window, duh. Mr. Nguyen's desk faces the other way, so you should have a perfect view of the computer screen from here."

"Is this illegal?"

"Why would it be? All we're doing is looking. Do they arrest people for looking these days?"

I sure hope not. I look at Elbie's skinny little arms and step back. "Hey, shouldn't I be holding you up? I *am* bigger."

"That's okay, get on."

"But it doesn't make sense."

"Okay, fine." He unclasps his hands. "The truth is, that kind of stuff scares me."

"What kind of stuff?"

"Being lifted up by someone. It makes me nervous." He threads his fingers together "Now would you get up there? We don't have all day."

Remembering all the things that bother me, I say, "Oh, okay," and rest my foot on his hands. "You sure this is going to work?"

"Heck yeah. Mr. Nguyen's out at the bus stop now. Just don't bang your head through the glass, and we'll be fine."

"Right." I whisper a quick prayer and stand on Elbie's hands. After a few wobbly moments, I've got my nose pressed to the window. Elbie's right. Mr. Nguyen's chair is empty.

"Can you see the screen?" Elbie asks.

"Yes, it's right there in front of me, just like you said."

"So? What's on it?"

"A horse. I think it's War Admiral. Or maybe Seattle Slew. It's hard to tell, since practically all racehorses are brown."

"A screensaver?"

"I think so."

"Well, that's no help. Can you see anything else?"

"Yes, Mr. Nguyen. Drop me. Drop me now."

Elbie's hands come apart. I fall and stumble backward a few steps until I get my balance.

"Time to go," I tell him. "It's hot, and I should be home by now."

"No, no, that can wait. Him being in there's a good thing. He'll probably get on his computer now." He shoves his hands back together and braces himself against the wall. "You want that bug book, don't you?"

"But what if he sees me?"

"He'll be sitting at his desk. There's no way he can see you."

Since that's probably true, I hop back on his hands, grab onto the window frame, and carefully pull myself up. Elbie's right. Mr. Nguyen is already sitting at his computer. I peer over his head. The screensaver is gone, replaced by words and a bunch of horses racing across the top of the screen.

"What's on the screen now?" Elbie asks.

I lean down and whisper, "I think he's looking at some kind of horseracing website." I peer back through the window as Mr. Nguyen jots something on his lime green notepad. His cell phone must be ringing, because he stops what he's doing and holds it to his ear. "He's talking on the phone. And writing. I wish I could hear what he's saying." Once Mr. Nguyen disconnects, he tears the paper off, reads it, then tosses it in his horse-covered wastebasket and starts over.

"What's he doing now?" Elbie asks.

"He's writing again."

"Writing what?" His voice sounds strained.

"I don't know. I didn't bring binoculars." I look down at him. His face is sweaty, and I don't think it's all because of the heat. "Are you getting tired?"

"Heck, yeah, I'm getting tired. You're not exactly a bag of feathers, you know."

I peer back through the window just as Miss Beverly enters Mr. Nguyen's office. I duck my head.

"Drop me, quick," I tell Elbie.

This time, he lowers his hands and I carefully hop down to the sidewalk.

"Did he get up again?"

"No, Miss Beverly came in. I think she's there to clean."

"Dang, this spying stuff is complicated." Still a little bent over, he shakes his hands and rubs them together. "Learn anything before she came in?"

"I'm not really sure. It would probably help if I knew what he was writing."

"That's easy. Just knock on his door and say hey, Mr. Nguyen, what were you writing a minute ago while I was watching you through the window?"

"But then, wouldn't he—wait . . . was that sarcasm?"

"Yes, that was sarcasm." Smiling, he straightens. "Don't worry, Jojo. I just figured out how to learn what Mr. Nguyen was writing."

ONCE ELBIE EXPLAINS his plan, we slip back into the building and head for the main office, both happy for the change to cooler air. Even at this hour, I can still smell the corndogs and tacos they served at lunchtime. As we hoped, Miss Beverly's little cart is still sitting outside. We dash toward it, but hit the brakes at the sound of her voice. Still talking, she steps out into the hallway, holding two wastebaskets, one of which has horses all over it.

"Yeah, that vacuum *is* pretty loud," she says to someone in the back area. "No problem. You and Mr. N. keep workin'. I'll clean in here later."

Before we can hide around the corner, she spots us. "Hey, guys. Did you find that sweatshirt you was lookin' for?"

Elbie grins and steps forward, his hands clasped behind his back. "Uh, no. We forgot. That's why we're here now. We came to check the lost and found."

She glances back into the office where Miss Juanita, her helmet of blond hair still perfectly in place, is typing away at her computer. "Hey, Juanita, mind checking the lost and found for Joey here? Seems he misplaced his sweatshirt."

"Sure," she calls back. "What color is it?"

Since I really did lose a sweatshirt a while back, I say, "Blue."

"Orange," Elbie says at the exact same time.

We step up to the counter.

"Well, which is it?" Miss Juanita asks. "Orange or blue?"

"Both," Elbie blurts. He drags his finger across his chest. "You know . . . stripes."

I stare, amazed at Elbie's ability to lie.

"Okay, orange and blue stripes," Miss Juanita says.

As she heads back to the lost and found cabinet, Elbie and I turn to watch as Miss Beverly dumps Mr. Nguyen's trash into the big yellow bag on her cart. A crumpled piece of lime green paper tumbles out of the wastebasket, and we both smile. But then comes another . . . and another.

"Sorry, no orange and blue sweatshirt there that I can see."

Miss Juanita's voice makes me jump. "Uh, that's okay." I try to think of something else to say. What I come up with is, "Stripes make my skin itch."

Both women chuckle, and I wonder if I should too. But too much time passes and Miss Juanita is already back at her computer.

"That's funny," Miss Beverly says, "but I thought you'd be more upset about not finding it. The way Elbie was talkin' yesterday, you'd be getting a whoopin' if you didn't come home with that sweatshirt." She tips her head of long gray hair to the side and looks right at me. Immediately, I decide my shoelaces need tightening.

"You know me. I tend to exaggerate." Elbie scans the tan linoleum for a few moments. "Hey, uh, didn't you just polish this floor the other day?" Face squashed up like he just chugged a cup of vinegar, he strides past the six principal portraits and stops in front of a long black heel mark. "It looks like you better bring your stick."

Miss Beverly all but drops the wastebaskets. I'm not surprised. Every kid in the school knows she's obsessed with keeping the floors spotless. Since black heel marks are her mortal enemy, she snatches her special tool from her cart, a broom handle with a tennis ball stuck to the end, and tromps over to where Elbie is pointing.

"Dang kids, it's like they do it on purpose." She presses the tennis ball to the floor and angrily scrubs at the marks.

With Miss Beverly focused on her linoleum, Elbie trots back to me and the cart. "Go on, start looking for those green papers. I'll keep her distracted."

While Elbie makes another black heel mark at the same time Miss Beverly is rubbing away at the old one, I reach into the garbage cart, then pull back. There's a half-eaten tuna fish sandwich slopped down at the bottom. Knowing I won't have another chance, I hold my breath and pull out every lime green paper I can find.

"Time to go," I tell Elbie as I stuff the last paper into my backpack.

He points out another scuffmark and stands by as Miss Beverly buffs it away. "Great work, Miss Beverly. Looks like you got them all. Wish I could stay and help, but Joey's right. We have a lot of reading to do."

"That's okay, Elbie. You're a good kid. Thanks for helping me out." She waves. "Bye, Joey. I sure hope your sweatshirt shows up."

CHAPTER 13

SINCE WE MIGHT need Theresa and Kerry's help figuring out Mr. Nguyen's notes, Elbie and I ride our bikes back to my house. The new air conditioning system works great and we breathe relieved sighs as cool air strikes our bodies. Like most Thursday afternoons, unfamiliar smells are coming from the kitchen. That's because Kerry is getting another of her cooking lessons. The giant butcher-block table Theresa bought with her prize money is dusted with flour, and she's watching Kerry flatten a wad of dough on it using Grandma Carmen's big fat rolling pin.

"What are you teaching her to make now?" Elbie asks her.

"A meat and vegetable pie," Theresa says. Seeing me, her eyes sparkle. "Hey, troublemaker. Did you ever figure out a way to get yourself sent to the principal's office?"

There's a tray filled with spice bottles on the table beside me. Still feeling a little guilty, I pick up a bottle and read the label.

Elbie chuckles. "Oh, he definitely did that." With lips curled into what I can best define as a smirk, he describes my prank to the girls, and they all but fall on the floor laughing.

A huge grin stretches across Theresa's face. "Holy crabs, Jojo. How did you come up with that?"

"You'd be surprised how many pranks people put on YouTube."

"Got that right," Elbie says, "And most are a heck of a lot harsher than what you pulled today. I probably deserved it anyway. Thanks for not gluing my butt to my chair, Jojo."

"Hey Elbie," Theresa says. "Have you seen our new refrigerator? Now that we've had the bathrooms remodeled, Dad let me pick one out. They delivered it yesterday, right after we got back from visiting the mortuary."

In the place of Grandma Carmen's ancient avocado-colored dinosaur sits a giant stainless-steel monster. Theresa opens one of its three doors and pulls out a pitcher. "Anybody want iced tea?"

"All that stuff was paid for with your *Ghosters* contest money?" Elbie asks her as she starts filling glasses.

Theresa looks back over her shoulder, a big grin on her face. "Sure did. I'd like to remodel the kitchen too, but my dad wants to wait. He says he'll need peace and quiet if he's going to finish his latest book on time."

Elbie shakes his head. "And all because of a few ghosts. That is so unfair. I see spirits every day, but my dad won't let me record them. He says it would bring in the wrong kind of people to the business."

"He's probably right," I tell him. From my backpack, I fish out the lime green papers I collected from Miss Beverly's trash cart and spread them on the counter.

Kerry raises the rolling pin from the dough's surface and peers over. "What's all that stuff?"

"They're from Mr. Nguyen's wastebasket."

"No way." Her flour-dusted face pinches. "You took them while he was in the same room?"

"It's a long story." Elbie waves his hand as if fanning the tale away. "What's important is what Mr. Nguyen wrote on them. We're hoping the words on one of these has something to do with Mrs. Cowan."

"Brilliant!" Hands dusty with flour, Kerry snatches one of the papers up by the corner. "Taco sauce . . . orange juice . . ." She drops it back onto the counter. "Doubt if an old grocery list is going to help us."

Elbie sips his tea as he reads another. "Ask Mom about her doctor's appointment."

"Humph. I guess even criminals have moms," Theresa says. "Come on, Kerry. Back to work. Let the boys sort through those."

As Theresa shows Kerry how to lay her crust into the pie pan, Elbie and I take turns reading aloud what's written on the rest of the papers. The one I get is a list of topics for his next faculty meeting, and the rest are equally as useless.

Elbie picks up the last sheet and chuckles. "Oh-my-God, check out this crazy list: Why kick a moo cow, your grandpa's moustache, electric cheeseburger, and Major Headache."

"I've heard illegal drugs sometimes have weird names," Theresa says. "Maybe Mr. Nguyen is on something. An addict can go through a ton of cash."

"Maybe he stole that grant money to pay for his habit." Kerry looks at me. "Did you notice any drugs when you were in there? Pills . . . needles?"

"No, not that I remember, but I didn't go through his drawers or anything."

"All right." Kerry scoops some sort of lumpy gravy-dripping concoction onto the bottom layer of crust. "So what *do* you remember seeing?"

Her pie filling reminds me of dog food, but I keep the thought to myself. Instead, I think back and try to remember all the things I saw when I was with Mr. Nguyen. "Horses. All over the place. I counted thirteen pictures of them. Some racing, some standing, some with flowers around their necks."

"Like those leis Hawaiian people wear?" Theresa says.

"Kind of. Even his wastebasket had horses on it."

"Yeah, I've seen all that," Elbie says. "But how does it help us with the ghost?"

"Crikey! I think I . . ." Kerry grabs Elbie's arm and snatches away the last sheet of paper.

After staring down at the strange list, she grins. "I may have figured out what all those words mean. If I'm right, Mr. Nguyen isn't on drugs. He's on horses."

"What are you talking about?" Theresa takes the paper away from Kerry.

"Why kick a moo cow . . . major headache. Are you saying these are all horse names?"

Although all of the horses in Mr. Nguyen's photos have odd names, some stand out in my mind. "Kerry could be on to something. Secretariat . . . Super Saver. There was even one called Gato del Sol. That's Cat of the Sun, in Spanish." I pick up the first paper I read. "So, why not taco sauce and orange juice? Could they be horses too?"

Kerry shrugs. "Totally possible. And if that's what they are, he wrote down their names because he was thinking of betting on them. The only way we'll know for sure is to find out where they might be running." She washes her hands, then pulls her cell phone out of her back pocket. "I'll search for racetracks near me." Her fingers tap and swipe. "There's a horseracing track at the Brimley Fairgrounds. That's about an hour's drive from here. Let's see if I can find out which horses will be running this weekend." After a few seconds, her eyes light up. "There they are, Your Grandpa's Moustache, Electric Cheeseburger . . . even Major Headache."

What about Taco Sauce and Orange Juice?" I ask. "Are they running too?"

She scrolls through the list. "No, but that doesn't mean they aren't horses." She looks at each of us and grins. "What's our next step?"

"How about finishing this pie?" Theresa says. "It's got to bake for at least an hour."

"Oh, relax. That crust won't take me that long." Kerry drops a second ball of pastry dough onto the table in front of her, and we all watch as she rolls it out. "See? Not bad for a beginner, right?"

As Theresa teaches Kerry how to mash the top and bottom layers of crust together with a fork, I summarize what we already know. "One, Mrs. Cowan got put in prison because Mr. Nguyen blamed her for taking the library's grant money."

They all nod.

"Two, Mrs. Cowan says she's innocent, and she died in prison."

Theresa sighs. "Probably of a broken heart."

"Maybe, but there's really no evidence of that," I say. "What we just learned is that after Mrs. Cowan specifically told us to visit Mr. Nguyen's office, we found out that he's super interested in horses and . . . ?"

"And he plans on betting on some. I mean, otherwise, why would the man write down those stupid names?" Elbie taps my arm. "Remember when you were peeking through his window? You said he was looking at some sort of horseracing website."

As Kerry walks her pie over to Grandma Carmen's old oven, Theresa gives me a shove. "You were peeping through that man's window?"

"Yes, but he didn't see me. Anyway, to answer Elbie's question, of course, I remember. It happened less than an hour ago. But I'm not really sure what Mr. Nguyen was looking at. All I know is there were pictures of horses running and the riders had funny clothes on just like Mr. Prendergast."

Theresa shakes her head. "Who's Mr. Prendergast?"

"A dead jockey." Elbie waves the question away. "But that's not important right now."

Theresa looks at me sideways.

"It really isn't." I wave my hand the way Elbie just did. "If Mr. Nguyen's addicted to gambling, then there's a good chance he'll be there to watch those horses race."

"We should go too," Elbie says. "There has to be a connection between his gambling and that grant money. If we go to the track, we can follow him around and maybe we'll learn what that is. Kerry, what day is all that happening?"

She scrolls down the screen some more, then grins. "This coming Saturday. Plus, there's a Harvest Fair going on too that day."

"What's that about?" Theresa asks.

"Hold on, I'll check." After doing some more tapping and swiping, Kerry says, "Okay, listen to this. 'Saturday, the city of Brimley celebrates their local farmers for the fifteenth year.' Then there's a list of what they're going to have. 'Over twenty food trucks serving dishes made from local crops, live music throughout the day, a livestock exhibit, horseracing at three . . . kids get in free, and . . . hold on . . .'" She looks up, a huge grin stretched across her face. "Anyone fancy carnivals?

"They're going to have rides too?" Elbie practically shouts.

"That's actually a perfect day trip," Theresa says. "We go to the fair, pet some bunnies, ride some rides, then go to the racetrack afterward."

"Yeah," Elbie says. "Nothing wrong with mixing business with pleasure, but how do we get our four butts to Brimley?"

CHAPTER 14

AS IT TURNS out, getting to the Brimley Harvest Fair is pretty easy. Dad loves stuff like that, so he's happy to go. Kerry's folks *were* planning on taking her to a wedding, but after some begging, she convinces them to let her come with us instead. And Mr. and Mrs. Bird surprise everyone. Not only are they going to the fair, but they're driving everyone else too. And best of all, we get to ride in that big black limo they use for funerals. Since the temperature is going to be in the high eighties, I wear shorts, but I also bring a towel to put between me and the car's leather seats.

Our plan is to see the attractions and ride the rides first. Then, because Elbie and Theresa think the grownups won't approve of us spying on Mr. Nguyen, we're going to find a way to ditch them and head over to the racetrack a few minutes before three, which is when the first race is supposed to start. There, we'll find Mr. Nguyen and watch him for a while. We all agree that he'll be betting on the horses, but we also suspect there's more to his trip here than just a little recreational betting.

Our folks pay for our tickets and we push through the turnstiles one by one. Before we take five steps, a man dressed like a scarecrow takes pictures of us and a smiling grandma-type woman wearing an old-time pioneer dress hands Dad and Mrs. Bird a fair guide. Even though the food concessions are at least a football field away, I can already smell the grease—and the corn dogs, which just happen to be one of my favorite foods.

"Okay kids, what do you want to do first?" Dad unfolds his fair guide and shows us all the bright cartoony map.

"I think we should start with the rides," Mr. Bird says, "before the lines get too long."

Everyone agrees, and we head on over to the ticket booth.

We all ride the Double Shot first. It's one of those tower rides that takes you up high and drops you like an out of-control-elevator. As we're slowly carried to the top of the tower I spot Mr. Bird's limo way out in the parking lot. Just as I open my mouth to say so, we start to drop, and as the ground races up to meet us, my stomach rises too. I hold my breath. Kerry and Theresa scream. So does Mrs. Bird, who I peer past to look at Elbie. As I expect, he's beaming that Tic Tac grin of his.

Across from the tower ride stands the Gravitron, my favorite. Before the grownups make it out onto the grass, we four kids are already in line.

With the two dads trailing her, Mrs. Bird joins us, head shaking. "I think I'll sit this one out. My stomach's a little queasy from the last ride."

Dad and Mr. Bird decide to skip it too, so it's just us kids. We step into the big metal cylinder, which is a lot like a giant hamster wheel that's fallen over. Standing side by side in our spots against the wall, we wait for the ride to start, hands anxiously gripping the rubber handles. Elbie is on my right and Theresa is on my left with Kerry beside her. Once everyone is in position, the whole thing starts spinning. Slowly, at first.

I notice a red-haired woman around our parents' age standing on the opposite side. As the ride picks up speed, her knuckles turn white as she grips the handles.

"See that white lady across from us?" Elbie asks me.

"You mean the one who looks like she's going to throw up?"

"Yeah." He grins. "I hope she does. That would be hilarious."

"I don't. The way this thing's spinning, there's a good chance her puke could land on us."

"Ew." Elbie's smile disappears. "I never thought of that."

Once the centrifugal force gets strong enough, it presses everyone to the wall, and the floor drops out from beneath us. But we couldn't fall if we tried. Heavy metal rock music has been playing the whole while with the volume increasing along with the speed of the ride. Lucky for me, I like rock music and don't need to cover my ears.

From the corner of my eye, I notice Elbie is moving around. I turn my head and watch as he battles the centrifugal force pressing down on him and rotates his skinny little body around until he's upside down. Across the wheel, some other kids are doing the same thing.

"You'd better turn right-side up before the ride ends!" I shout over the music. "If you don't, you'll fall on your head when this thing slows down!" I must scare him because he turns right-side up a few moments later.

"Hey!" Theresa taps me. "Look!"

I follow her gaze. Six spaces to our right is a tall thin man dressed in suede pants and matching jacket with fringe along the outside of his sleeves, a lot like the jacket Ms. Skyeblu had on the other day. "With that raccoon cap, he looks just like that famous explorer guy . . ." Theresa's eyebrows push together as she pauses.

"I think you mean Daniel Boone!" Elbie hollers.

"That's the guy!" Theresa says. She turns to me and smiles. "Bet you wouldn't want a hug from old Daniel Boone over there, huh, Jojo? All that leather . . . ?"

As she waits for my response, the explorer notices I'm looking at him and nods. Since that's another way of saying hello, I nod back. But then he begins to fade out. Daniel Boone is a ghost. Unable to hold his realistic appearance for more than a few seconds, the fringy leather clothes are now transparent.

"Hey, Theresa. Look again!" Elbie says.

"And hurry!" I say, voice raised so my sister will hear. "He's like an oil painting that just turn into a watercolor!"

"What are you guys talking about?" Kerry shouts from the other end.

"Yeah, what?" Theresa glances back at the explorer. "Holy crabs, Kerry, that Daniel Boone guy was a ghost."

Kerry looks where we're looking. "What Daniel Boone guy?"

"He was right there!" Theresa points. "Next to that kid with the yellow tee-shirt!"

"Arrrg!" Kerry moans. "Another ghost! This is so unfair!"

It is unfair. Kerry likes ghosts more than any of us and she's the only one who can't see them without some sort of camera. I look back at the now empty spot and wonder if the ghost is actually gone. And why is he here, anyway? Did he come to enjoy the carnival, or is he attached to this place because it's where he died. And how long ago was that? One hundred years? Two? All good questions, but ones I'm not likely to learn the answer to.

We rotate a dozen more times before the Gravitron comes to a complete stop. As soon as it does, the woman across from us races out, her face damp and pasty.

"I sure hope she finds a garbage can," Elbie mutters. "The way my luck has been going, if she ralphs on the grass, I'll probably step in it."

"You have been a little clumsy," I say, then turn to the others. "What should we ride now?"

We settle on the bumper cars, and this time, all three parents join us. After that, we get something to eat—a giant corndog for me—then ride The Paratrooper, The Octopus, and some other rides with names I can't remember. Sometimes the parents join us, but mostly they don't.

Around two-thirty, we find the grownups sitting on a bench watching a magic show.

"Hey," Mr. Bird says, glancing down at his fair guide. "There's a jazz quartet playing in the bandshell at three o'clock. You kids want to go, or will you be okay without us for an hour or so?"

We all look at each other. Three o'clock is when the horses start racing.

"That's perfect," I tell him. "Three o'clock is also—"

"A perfect time to check out the farm animals," Elbie pipes up. He turns to his mom. "You don't want to go there, anyway, right? Not with your allergies."

Animals? What happened to going to the racetrack? I look at Theresa, who gives me a barely noticeable headshake. I think she wants me to be quiet.

"Then, we're settled." Dad points at the big flag pole a few yards away. "Meet us over there around four." He passes Theresa some money.

Elbie gets some from Mrs. Bird, and after promising to stay together, we run off toward the big red barn.

"I thought we were going to the racetrack," I tell Theresa.

"We still are." She stops and looks back the way we came. "Kerry, you're taller. Can you still see the folks?"

"No sight of them."

"Great," Elbie says. "The racetrack is to the left."

As we follow the girls, I ask Elbie why we couldn't just leave Mr. Nguyen out of the story and tell our parents we were going to the track.

"We could," he answers, "but come on, dawg. Isn't it more fun to be sneaky? It's like we're spies on a secret mission. You know, James Bond stuff."

"James Bond gets into dangerous situations."

"Well not that, but—"

"People shoot at him all the time."

"Would you two stop lagging," Theresa calls back to us. "Hustle up. The track is way on the other side of the fairgrounds."

The wide freshly painted path takes us straight through the Midway, sort of a car-free street lined with carnival games on both sides. First there's the Whack a Mole. Next to that is the game where you throw darts at balloons and beyond that are people squirting water into a clown's mouth.

"Hang on a sec," Elbie says, eyeing a booth decorated with giant stuffed frogs. "I want to try this basketball toss game."

"Are you kidding?" Kerry says. "All of these games are rigged."

As I try to figure out what rigged means, a skinny man with a Mickey Mouse tattoo peeking out the top of his tee-shirt calls us over. Elbie goes, and the rest of us follow.

The stall the man's working in has three basketball hoops and is layered with giant stuffed frogs. "Three throws for two dollars!" the tattooed man announces loudly. He bounces the red, white, and blue basketball a few times, then tosses it to Elbie. "One shot. That's all you have to make."

"What does rigged mean?" Elbie whispers in my ear.

"I don't know, but look at the diameter of the rim. It's a lot smaller than normal."

Kerry bends low to whisper in Elbie's ear. "See? Rigged."

"Oh, yeah." He tosses back the ball. "Sorry, I've decided to save my money."

As the four of us walk down the midway, more carnival barkers call out to us from all directions. With so many voices coming at me, I find myself walking slower, and it's not just me. At the sight of all the colorful stuffed prizes they offer, even Kerry's pace slows. Everywhere we look, there's something cool to win: giant Sponge Bobs, grinning monkeys riding giant bananas, even a five-foot-tall purple gorilla. I'd love to win something for each of us, but Kerry is probably right.

"Come on," I tell Theresa when she stops to stare at a giant pink and purple stuffed unicorn. "The first race starts in fifteen minutes, and we still haven't found Mr. Nguyen."

CHAPTER 15

THE GRANDSTAND MUST be more elevated than the rest of the fair, because I can already see it, even though we're still on the midway. Rippling waves of heat rise from the wide blacktop path leading up to the racetrack. I'm relieved to spot the big roof shading the bleachers and a sign advertising pink lemonade and iced tea. But we can't just walk in. There's a tall wire fence surrounding the entire racetrack area, and a line of people backed up in front of the ticket booth.

"I didn't know we'd have to pay to get in," I tell Theresa.

"Remember? Kids get in free." There's a sign next to the ticket window that none of us can read from the back of the line. Theresa runs over to check it out, then jogs back.

"What's wrong?" Elbie says. "You look like my dad the time I asked him why Tarzan doesn't have a beard."

"We're sunk," Theresa says, ignoring Elbie's remark. "I was right about kids getting in free, but they have to be accompanied by an adult."

"What do we do now?" I ask her. "Dad won't want to leave the concert."

"Neither will my folks," Elbie says.

Kerry shades her eyes and looks the fence up and down. "We could try climbing over."

"We could, but hang on a sec." Elbie turns his back to the racetrack and strokes his chin thoughtfully as he studies the crowd of people trudging up the slope toward us and the grandstand. "What would James Bond do?" he murmurs.

Since I'm pretty sure he's just talking to himself, I don't answer, and after a bit, Elbie takes off running down the hill.

"What's he doing?" Theresa asks me.

"I'm not sure, but I think it's something James Bond would do."

About a dozen yards down, Elbie stops in front of a couple around Dad's age. The woman is pushing a baby stroller. They have another kid too, a girl, but a lot younger than Elbie and me.

Elbie says something to the mom as they all stroll toward us and the grandstand. The dad says something and Elbie points back at the rest of us. They shade their eyes, then wave. The three of us wave back. After the dad and mom talk a little, they both look at Elbie and nod. Ten seconds later, Elbie and his new friends are standing right in front of us.

"So," the man turns to Kerry, "Elbie here says you're visiting from England, and you've never seen a horserace."

For a moment, Kerry stands there, but then she suddenly smiles. "Oooh, yeah. Never have."

"See?" Elbie says. "Kerry's visiting her American cousins. Joey and Theresa, say hi to Mr. And Mrs. Everett. They've offered to escort us into the racetrack."

"You sure your parents are okay with you going in there without them?" Mrs. Everett asks. Her rosy cheeks are shiny with sweat.

"We're sure," Elbie says. "My folks stayed at the fair because my mom's allergic to horses."

Once we promise not to get into any trouble, Mr. Everett pays for their admission tickets and we all push through the turnstile and into the racetrack area.

"Why *doesn't* Tarzan have a beard?" I ask Elbie as we enter the shaded area beneath the grandstand. "Don't all men have some form of facial hair? And if he *does* shave, where would he get the razor?"

"That's one of those mysteries with no answer," Elbie tells me. "Like how come scientists got a man on the moon before they figured out how to put wheels on a suitcase."

Before I can consider the suitcase mystery, Theresa gives both of us a shove in the back. "Be quiet you guys and look around. Mr. Nguyen is probably here already."

"Relax," Elbie tells her. "Our eyes are wide open."

"Why would we close them?" I ask him. Instead of answering, Elbie squints up at the sky.

"By the way," Kerry says. "What does this Nguyen fellow look like? From the name, I imagine he's Vietnamese, but what else?"

"He slicks back his hair." Elbie drags his hand across his own super-short cut. "And it's black."

I nod. "And he's not as tall as you or my dad."

"My dad either," Elbie adds. "And he wears suits all the time. One is dark blue, another is—"

"We get it," Theresa interrupts. "But principals wear suits because they're at work. I doubt if he'll be wearing one at the racetrack."

I look around at the mass of people swarming around us like bees on a hive. She's right. Except for the really old men who have on slacks, most are wearing shorts and tee-shirts.

It smells like stale beer under the grandstand, but at least we're in the shade. Kerry picks up a leaflet with pictures of houses on it, then uses it to fan herself as we scan our surroundings. The place is a long rectangle, about the length of three classrooms with one of the longer walls open like a big doorway. Across is a row of food and drink concessions. On one short side of the rectangle are seven windows with people lined up in front of them, sort of like at a bank or movie theater. The sign above them says Betting and Cashing. On the opposite wall are the restrooms.

"Tell you what," Kerry says, still fanning herself. "You boys keep looking for your Mr. Nguyen, and Theresa and I will go buy us some lemonade."

After a few minutes, I still haven't seen anyone who even looks like Mr. Nguyen. Neither has Elbie. He pulls out his cell phone and checks the time. "Five minutes before the first race. Maybe we're looking in the wrong area. If he already placed his bet, he's probably in the stands by now."

Elbie nudges me. "Check out the guy at the end of line number one."

I glance over. "How could you think that's Mr. Nguyen? He's not even Asian."

"I realize that. Look harder."

I turn back around. "Hey, he keeps fading in and out."

"Uh huh. Another watercolor ghost. Check out that suit and fedora he's wearing."

"What's a fedora?"

"His hat. That there is an old-school gangster. You know, like in those old black and white movies."

As Elbie and I stare, the man in front of the ghost frowns at his phone screen then angrily elbows his friend.

"Uh oh," Elbie whispers. "Looks like Mr. Gangster's been draining the juice out of that dude's phone."

As if sensing he's being watched, the slowly fading ghost turns toward us and tips his hat.

"What do we do now?" I whisper.

"This." Elbie raises one hand and waves.

Since it would be impolite not to, I wave too. "I wonder why these ghosts haven't . . . you know . . . moved on."

"Who knows? They could be scared to go. Heck, maybe this guy won a lot of money here and doesn't want to leave."

From the other end of the building, we spot Kerry and Theresa walking toward us, each of them carrying two paper cups.

I glance back at line number one. As I expect, the gangster is gone. "Should we tell them about the ghost?"

"What for? Theresa doesn't like them and Kerry will just get mad since she missed it and wouldn't have seen it anyway."

"Any luck?" Theresa asks. She passes me a straw and a cup of lemonade beaded with condensation. I surprise myself by chugging down half of it.

"None," Elbie says as he pays Kerry for the drink she brought him. He pulls the wrapper from his straw, but instead of dropping the paper in the nearby wastebasket, he tucks it in his pocket.

"What's that for?" I ask him.

"You'll see."

Besides the drinks, Theresa brings back a long narrow pamphlet. "This should help us. It's called a racing form. It lists every horse in each of the ten races. Cost three dollars too."

She passes it to me, and I turn to the first page. "Thanks, sis. I'll pay you back when we get home."

"No worries. That twenty bucks Dad gave me was for both of us, remember?"

As we enter the tunnel leading out to the track, the sound of a trumpet blasts over the loudspeaker. It's the same tune Mr. Prendergast asked to be played at his funeral service.

"We better hustle," Elbie tells us. "That means the first race is going to start."

We walk faster, and soon we're back out in the baking sunshine. Between the grandstand and the white plastic railing that surrounds the track is a wide blacktopped walkway. There are several people standing against the railing. Some holding binoculars, most wearing sunglasses or hats.

Elbie bumps me with his shoulder. "Check out that lady in the white dress."

I follow his gaze. Standing against the railing is a tall slender woman with curly blond hair. Her dress has no back, and her tan skin stands out against the bright whiteness of the dress. Beside her is a dark-skinned man wearing a red baseball cap. "So, what? She's really tan?"

"Wait for it." He pulls the straw out of his drink and grins. "And don't say anything when it happens."

Since I have no idea what Elbie is planning, I turn to see what Theresa and Kerry are doing. They're staring up into the stands, hands shading their eyes. I do it too, but I also want to see what Elbie is up to, so I keep glancing over my shoulder.

The grandstand is shaded with at least twenty rows of seats, and most of them are full. The back row is way up high, but not so far away that I can't see the peoples' faces. As far as I can tell, none of them belongs to Mr. Nguyen.

I check on Elbie. Like every other time I've looked back at him, he's still focused on the lady in the white dress. Wondering why Elbie's so interested in her, I move closer.

"Here goes. Now remember, don't react." Elbie fills his cheeks with air, holds the drink straw to his lips, and blows.

With a splat, the spitball hits the woman's bare back. In a knee-jerk reaction, she squeals and her shoulder blades pull together. Grinning, Elbie quickly turns his back to the woman, the straw already tucked in his cup.

"Look away," he hisses. "You want to get us in trouble?" He peers up at the stands, the grin suddenly replaced by a look of peaceful boredom.

I turn too and look at him from the corner of my eye. "Why would *I* get in trouble? *You're* the one who shot the spit wad at her."

"Yeah, but if you keep staring at her, she'll think it was you." He turns back to study the horses, which are just stepping onto the track. "Okay, you can look, but just be subtler about it."

Subtler? Head still down, I sneak a quick look at the woman. The man with the baseball cap is wiping her back with a napkin and glaring at the crowd around them.

"Theresa leans in. "Hey, Jojo, what just happened to that lady?"

"I . . ."

"Someone shot her in the back with a spitball," Elbie says.

Her eyes narrow. "Someone?"

He sips his drink and shrugs. "What about Mr. Nguyen? You find him yet?"

"Not yet," Theresa says. "This place is packed."

She's right. And for me, at least, it's not easy to keep my focus with so much going on. The horses are closer now, all wearing foot-tall numbers the same bright colors as the jockeys. Seeing they're going to pass right by us, the four of us crowd against the railing to get a better look.

If you don't count the footprints and occasional lumps of fresh horse poop, the rust colored dirt is silky smooth, and as the horses pass by us, their hooves puff it up in little clouds. This close, I can smell their sweat, as well as their poop. But I don't mind. They're not the worst things I've ever smelled.

"I like the scent of fresh dirt," Elbie tells me.

"Me too. But it's not really the dirt smell we like so much, it's actually a creature called a geosmin, a form of bacteria that lives *in* the dirt. I read that in the *Five Senses* book too."

Not sure how to interpret the look Elbie gives me, I open the racing form to check the names of the horses in the first race and spot one from Mr. Nguyen's list. "Your Grandpa's Moustache is in the first race," I tell Elbie.

He nudges me with his shoulder. "I'm sure that's true, but do you have any idea how stupid you sound saying it?"

"It's not my fault his owner named him that. It's number six if you're interested."

"Look, there he is now." Kerry points at a gray horse with a black mane and tail.

"Your Grandpa's Moustache." Elbie chuckles. "I don't know if he's fast, but he sure is the right color."

As Kerry watches the jockey struggle to get his horse over to the starting gate, her mouth turns downward. "He doesn't appear eager to join his friends, does he?"

She's right. The other nine horses are already lined up in their little metal stalls. All except number six, which is also the same number of men it takes to shove Your Grandpa's Moustache into position. Once the door shuts behind him, a bell rings and all ten of the front gates fly open at once. The horses bolt out, dashing down the track, hooves thundering. Immediately, the people in the stands start shouting. A man's voice bursts from a loudspeaker and describes what we're watching over the roar of the crowd.

The pack rumbles past us with Sausage King, the number two horse, leading the way and Your Grandfather's Moustache bringing up the rear.

"Maybe he's just a slow starter," Kerry says.

The four of us lean against the railing as the horses circle the track. In the end, a horse called Teddy's Dream wins, and Your Grandfather's Moustache is dead last.

"Man," Elbie says. "I sure feel sorry for anybody who bet on that horse."

"If we're right, that would be Mr. Nguyen," I say and turn back to look at the grandstand to find that several people are getting up and walking back down the tunnel. "I thought there were more races. Where are all those people going?"

"Probably to place another bet." Kerry studies the little racing form Theresa bought earlier and waves for us to follow. "Come on. Why Kick a Moo Cow is running in the second race. Let's go back to the betting area and see if we can spot that principal of yours."

CHAPTER 16

AS IT TURNS out, Kerry's grandmother took her to quite a few horseraces back when Kerry lived in England. "If they do things the same way here in the states, there should be a twenty-minute break between races. They do that so people have plenty of time to place their bets or get something to eat."

Elbie suggests we break off into two groups so as not to stick out as much. Since he and I know exactly what Mr. Nguyen looks like, we post ourselves near the betting windows while the girls are in charge of watching the rest of the crowd.

After a while, the area clears out with still no sign of Mr. Nguyen. Kerry waves us over. "The second race is going to start soon. Let's go search the stands again."

We go back out to the front area and walk to the end of the grandstand as the horses are being lead to the starting gate.

"Why Kick a Moo Cow is wearing number eight," Kerry tells us.

"I see him," Theresa says. "He's the white one with the big brown spots."

"Like a moo cow." Elbie chuckles.

During the race, we all search the seats. Kerry and Theresa point out two Asian men with slicked back hair, but one's too fat and the other is way too thin.

The spotted horse doesn't do much better than the gray one, and we head back to the betting area after Why Kick a Moo Cow comes in fifth. The jazz band will finish playing in fifteen minutes, so this is our last chance to locate Mr. Nguyen. Again, Kerry and Theresa stand near the concessions, and Elbie and I position ourselves in front of the ticket windows.

We're barely there two minutes when Elbie says, "Too much lemonade. I gotta pee."

As the men's room door closes behind Elbie, I spot Mr. Nguyen. Instead of a suit, he's wearing knee-length cargo shorts, a blue and white Hawaiian shirt, and some sort of black leather bag tied around his waist. Topped off with a big floppy hat and mirrored sunglasses, it's no wonder I barely recognize him. Mr. Nguyen must have also drunk too much lemonade, because he's headed for the men's room too.

I run over to the girls. "I know where Mr. Nguyen is now."

"Yeah?" Theresa turns and stands on tiptoes as she scans the lines below the betting windows. "Which line is he in?"

"He's not in a line. At least I don't think so. There could be one inside the men's room."

"That's okay." Kerry waves us over to one of the concrete pillars that hold up the stands. "We'll just wait right here and watch the door until he comes out."

"Where's Elbie?" Theresa says.

"In the men's room with Mr. Nguyen."

"What?"

"Don't worry," Kerry says. "If there's one thing Elbie's good at, it's making up a believable story."

As we watch people go in and out of the men's room, I begin to wonder if Kerry's description of Elbie isn't a compliment. But my thoughts are interrupted when the door swings open, and Elbie comes dashing out. I wave my arms, and he runs over.

"I saw Mr. Nguyen go into the men's room," I tell him. "Did he see you?"

Elbie shakes his head. "No, but it was close. I turned around, and there he was, standing in front of the mirror, washing his hands. Man, I thought I was going to have a heart attack. Lucky for me, these two guys came in and started talking to him. Dawg, that principal did not look happy to see them. I ran out while he was still distracted."

"That could be important," Theresa says. "What did the men look like?"

"Hmmm. Let me think." Elbie's lips pucker. "Thugs. And definitely younger than him. The big Asian one had on baggy jeans and a long black tee. The little white guy was wearing super long jean shorts and a wife-beater undershirt."

I tap his shoulder. "Are you saying there are undershirts specifically designed for abusive husbands?"

Elbie blinks. "Abusive husbands? Who said anything about—?"

"Forget the shirts!" Theresa says, more loudly than necessary. "Did you hear what they were talking about?"

"I don't know. Money, I think."

As we're standing there talking, Mr. Nguyen steps out of the men's room closely followed by the two men Elbie just described. The one wearing the white undershirt points to his right and shoves Mr. Nguyen, who starts to walk faster.

"Gross," Theresa says. "You didn't mention your principal is wearing a fanny pack."

"I didn't know the name," I tell her. "Was it important? What do we do now?"

Without answering, Elbie takes off after the men.

"Looks like we follow," Kerry says.

We trail the three men out to the far side of the racetrack and the fence that surrounds it. There's another entrance there, and a little silver-haired man is working the ticket booth. Mr. Nguyen and the other two men exit through the metal rotating gate nearby and head off through the parking lot.

"Those gates only rotate one way," Theresa says. "We'll be stuck out there."

"Not if we get our hands stamped," Elbie says.

We all jog over to the old man. One by one he stamps our hands, and we push our way through the exit gate.

"Okay, now which way did they—?"Kerry stops in her tracks. "Wait . . . is that them up there?"

We all shrug.

"There . . ." She stabs the air with her finger. "Two rows over . . . by that red Mustang." She starts to run, but Elbie whisper-shouts her back.

"Not that way," he tells her. "If we stay one row over, there's less chance they'll see us, and we'll still be moving in the same direction."

Everyone agrees, and as we trot past car after car, I wonder which police show Elbie stole his idea from. After a bit, Elbie slows to a walk and holds one finger to his lips. The three men are standing behind a black SUV. Waving his hands as he talks, Mr. Nguyen speaks quickly, a disturbing-looking grin stretched across his face. After rattling on for a while, he holds up one hand for a high five, but neither man slaps it, and the principal ends up looking like he's doing a Hitler salute.

"I think he's scared of them," I say, a little proud that I remembered to whisper. "I wish we could hear what they're saying."

"Let's move closer," Elbie says. "We'll use that big white van for cover."

Crouching low, he scurries between the parked cars into the next row, and the rest of us follow, keeping the white van between us and the three men. While we're creeping, I hear a dull thump, followed by a loud groan. I peek around the van and gasp.

The others make similar noises when they see Mr. Nguyen lying on the ground, his hands covering his nose. His sunglasses and big floppy hat are lying a few feet away. "Why'd you punch me?" he whines through bloody red fingers. "I told you I'd have the money next week."

The man with the white undershirt must not believe him. He bends over Mr. Nguyen and stuffs both hands into the fanny pack, pulls out a wallet and a thick wad of bills.

"Why you little liar," he growls, giving Mr. Nguyen a kick. "There's at least five hundred here. Back in the john, you said you lost everything in the first two races."

Nguyen raises both hands as if ready to block another punch. "Sorry, sorry. I was wrong to lie to you. I know that now." As Nguyen slowly sits up, a bead of nose blood drops ignored onto the front of his Hawaiian shirt. "It's just that I've got this sure thing in the fifth race," he sputters. "M-major Headache. He's ten to one, but the trainer's a friend of mine, and he promised me that if—"

The now empty wallet bounces off his face, cutting off his words.

"See my friend here?" The smaller man points. "He's going to keep an eye on you. If he catches you making any more bets today, it's you who's gonna have a major headache. Now go home. And get me that money some other way. Your next payment is due the eighteenth."

"Like I don't know that," Nguyen mutters.

The men walk off as Mr. Nguyen picks up his hat and sunglasses.

"Blast," Kerry says. "We should have recorded it."

Elbie slaps his hand to his forehead. "Why didn't I think of that?"

"You were too engrossed in watching your principal get beat up," I tell him. "We all were. And that's a shame because a picture really is worth a thousand warts."

"Words," Theresa tells me. "A thousand words."

I look at my watch. "Whatever. We need to get back to the carnival. Our folks wanted us back at the flagpole five minutes ago."

IT'S HARD FOR me to carry on a conversation while I'm running, so I don't say much as the others discuss what to tell the parents. What we all agree on is that Mr. Nguyen's gambling problem must be really bad if he's getting beat up over it.

It takes us ten minutes to get to the flagpole. Dad and Mr. and Mrs. Bird are sitting on a bench, all wearing the same expression.

"Where have you been?" Dad says. "We've been waiting fifteen minutes."

Kerry steps forward, hands clasped in front of her. "Sorry, Mr. Martinez. You can blame me for that. The line for the giant slide was super long."

"They don't have those slides in England," Elbie says.

"We were getting worried." Mrs. Bird hooks her purse strap on her shoulder and stands up. "But as long as you kids are all right. Ready to go home now?"

The others say they are, and I agree, even though we never got to see the animals.

The parents lead the way, followed by us kids. As we stroll back to the limo, we hang back a little so the grownups can't hear us talking.

"Okay, so he bets on racehorses," Theresa says. "And he owes some people a lot of money."

"And from the way those two thugs treated him," Kerry says, "I doubt this is the first time he's struggled to pay them back."

"Oh, heck no," Elbie says. "That's probably why he stole that grant money, so he could pay off his loans. But he couldn't quit betting, and now he owes them more."

That makes a lot of sense. What I don't understand is why Mr. Nguyen keeps getting himself into trouble. Why keep betting if all you do is lose?

"Okay," Theresa says. "We know it's Mr. Nguyen who stole the money, and we're pretty sure why he stole it. But how are we going to prove all that?"

"We have to tell Mrs. Cowan," Elbie says. "Maybe she knows what to do."

"If it's okay with you guys," I say, "I'd rather not use that pencil trick again. Especially after what happened the last time."

CHAPTER 17

THE DAY AFTER our trip to the racetrack, Elbie calls me, a strange tone to his voice. "I need your help. Please, come over."

Normally, that much drama would make me suspicious, but since I don't have anything better to do, I head over anyway. As usual, I park my bike alongside the limo and climb up the back stairs. Once inside, Skunky the cat greets me by sharpening his claws on my pant leg. Elbie shoos the cat away, and we head up to his room. Too bad Skunky follows.

"I think there's something wrong with me," Elbie says. He crawls up onto his unmade bed and with his back against the headboard, hugs his knees to his chest. Suddenly, he looks more like five than ten and a half.

"What are you talking about?"

"I'm always tripping over things. My shoelaces . . . my toys . . ."

I look around. As usual, there are at least twenty Legos strewn across the carpet. Mixed into the mess are two empty video game boxes, his skateboard, and various heaps of clothing along with a minimum of twenty steelies, cat's eyes, and swirls, two of which, Skunky has just batted under the bed. "Maybe you should clean up a little."

"Yeah, but being clumsy isn't all I'm worried about. I keep forgetting where I put things. My TV remote. The game controllers. Plus, my fly is always open." His eyebrows push together. "I think I'm losing my marbles."

"Well, Skunky just knocked some under your bed. If you put them back in their box when you're finished—"

"Not those marbles, dawg. I'm talking about my mind."
As Elbie worries about going crazy, Skunky hops up on the
bed between me and my friend and stares, as if daring me
to sit.

"Maybe you just need to slow down," I say. "Try double-
checking your pants before you leave the bathroom."

"That's what's crazy, because I specifically remember
zipping up, but not long after, it's down again."

"Are you sure it's not the zipper's fault?"

"It's not just one pair of pants, man. It's all of them, long
and short." Elbie stretches out his legs, and immediately,
Skunky hops onto his chest and lies down, their faces
separated by inches.

Not sure what else to say, I go with, "What do your
parents think?"

"They said what you said. Clean your room better
and slow down." He stares blankly up at the ceiling as he
scratches the cat behind its ears.

I've never seen Elbie like this. Keeping my distance from
Skunky, I sit on the end of the bed and say, "Maybe you
just need to take your mind off it. We could play ping pong
again."

Elbie wraps his arms around Skunky and raises his head
to look at me. "You serious? I thought you didn't like going
down there."

"I don't, but if your dad's not napping . . ."

"Actually, he's out of town on business. But ping pong
sounds good." Smiling, Elbie pushes the cat onto the bed,
jumps up, and falls to the floor. "See?" he half cries. "That's
the third time I tripped over the skateboard this week! Now,
do you understand? This stuff happens all the time."

That definitely is strange. "Wasn't it over by the door
when we first came in?"

He sits up and rubs his knee. "Man, I don't know anything
anymore." He pulls his cell phone out of his back pocket,
scowls down at it, then tosses it across the bed. "Dead. That

stupid phone is another thing that's been ticking me off. It probably needs a new battery."

Elbie threatens to toss both phone and battery into the wastebasket, but I convince him to try charging it one more time, and we head downstairs. Definitely not his normal playful self, Elbie walks right past the casket room without asking me if I'd like to try one out. At the bottom of the basement stairs we turn left into the storage room. Like before, Mr. Bird's golf clubs are lying on the ping pong table. Elbie drags them off and props them against the shelf, alongside the boxes filled with unwanted ashes.

"Okay. Time to get whooped." Elbie dashes toward the table, then stops. The red paddle is lying on the far side along with one white ping pong ball. "Did you hide the black paddle?"

"Why would I do that?"

We both peer under the table, then turn slow circles. No black paddle. Elbie tosses up his hands. "See? It's happening again."

"I can see why you're upset, but I really don't think you're insane. Normal people misplace things all the time. My dad always says, 'If something's not where it's supposed to be, then look where it's *not* supposed to be.'"

He tips his head to the side. "Where? Like upstairs in the fridge?"

"I would explore down here more before we start searching your mom's vegetable drawers." I wave him away. "You go check in the other room. I'll explore this one some more."

Elbie agrees and heads off to the embalming room. Working with the theory that the paddle may have fallen between some nearby suitcases, I move them around. No paddle. I squeeze behind two barrels of chemicals to the three caskets stacked against the far wall. They're all covered with bubble wrap with another layer of shrink-wrapped plastic over that. I peer behind them, on top. Again, no paddle. I search Mr. Bird's workbench too, but it's the same thing. Where else could that paddle be?

Since Mr. Bird's big black barbeque is right next to the suitcases, I lift the lid, just in case. But, besides the smell of burnt barbeque sauce, there's nothing in there but ashes.

Ashes?

I head over to the metal storage rack with all the little boxed up dead people on them. Some shelves hold three boxes, others four. All are covered with dust and cobwebs except for one down at the bottom. I bend down for a better look. Leaning against it is Elbie's black ping pong paddle. I pick it up and call him back into the room.

"Where was it?"

"Down there."

He crouches beside the shelves and peers at the box. "That's weird. Nobody's played ping pong since you spent the night. I smell a ghost."

"Really?"

Ignoring my sniffing, Elbie picks up the paddle and stands up. "I don't get it. Why would a ghost take my paddle?"

"Why do *you* like to play pranks?"

He tilts his head. "You think it's playing a prank on me?"

"Why not? Mr. Prendergast enjoyed making me jump. If I'm right, it would sure explain all the other weird things that have been happening to you."

"So, all this time some ghost has been untying my shoelaces and moving my stuff around?"

I shrug. "It would also explain why your phone is always dead. Does any of this stuff happen to you when you *aren't* here at the mortuary?"

He narrows his eyes. "Yeah, but ghosts can attach themselves to people. Follow them wherever they go. What I want to know is *who* the comedian is." He peers through the doorway in the direction of the embalming room. "Hey, you, the ghost who's been messing with me. Show yourself."

Nothing happens.

Having never seen Elbie so angry, I watch as he marches into the embalming room. Feet set wide, he stands in front of the stainless-steel wall of drawers.

"Somebody in here got a problem with me?" he shouts. "If you do, come on out and tell me about it!"

Wondering how many clients are in the home today, I forget my search for the paddle and watch. It doesn't take long. As Elbie continues to call out the ghost, a tall thickset man wearing dirty jeans and no shirt manifests behind him.

The man raises one of his beefy tattooed arms and taps Elbie on the shoulder. "Hey kid, knock off the noise."

Elbie spins and tips his head back to look at the giant ghost. "Fuh-finally."

"It wasn't us," the ghost says.

"Wha-what?" Elbie stammers.

The ghost raises his chin at the human filing cabinet behind Elbie. "Us. Them. None of the folks in those drawers have been bothering you."

"Then who has?"

"I got no clue." The ghost crosses his arms, covering what I'm thinking is a bullet hole on his chest. "But if you keep up that racket, I *am* gonna mess with you." He glides past Elbie and lays a big hand on one of the stainless-steel doors. "This here's me. I know I'm not buried yet, but I'd like to start with the rest in peace stuff right now. That okay with you?"

Elbie's eyes go wide. "Sure, I . . . okay."

The big man vanishes, and Elbie trots back to where I am. "Geez, scary guy."

"You were pretty loud."

"Okay, well, I said I'd stop yelling. But what about the comedian? If it's not one of them," he points back at the embalming room, "then who is it, and what do they want from me?"

I walk back to the shelves stacked with twenty or so shoebox-sized containers. "What about these people?"

He steps up beside me. "What about them?"

"Can't one of *them* be responsible?"

He looks the shelves up and down. "I guess it's possible, but if any of those ghosts are still here, I wouldn't know. Remember? Cremated ghosts can't manifest."

"Yeah, just like Mrs. Cowan." I pick up one of the boxes and read the age-yellowed tag, "This one's been sitting here since 1981. It's sad that their families didn't want to take them. Are they just going to sit here forever?"

"Probably."

"But what happens to . . . to *them*?"

"You mean their spirits?" He shrugs. "They move on, I guess. My dad says ghosts only stick close to their body until they get used to being dead. After that . . ." He looks up at the ceiling.

"They go to the lobby?"

"Not upstairs, man. To heaven."

"All of them?"

"Well, yeah, if they aren't headed for the other place. Like I said, if it's any different with the cremated guys, I sure don't know."

I crouch down in front of the dusty shelf where I found the ping pong paddle. Unlike all the other boxes which have yellow faded labels, the box that had the paddle leaning against it looks brand new. I tip it back so I can read the bright orange sticker glued to its front.

This is a Temporary Container for the Cremated Remains of
Name <u>Marvin Woodrow</u>
Cremated <u>October10th, 2016</u>
Cremation No. <u>5817</u>
Virtue Funeral Home

"October tenth. This one's only been here a couple of weeks. Isn't that how long this stuff has been happening to you?" I ask Elbie.

"Yeah, it is, and if this Woodrow guy's responsible, it sure would explain a lot of the weird stuff that's been happening." Elbie crouches beside me and slides the box off the shelf and onto the floor in front of us. "Marvin Woodrow. I don't remember him at all." He taps the name with his finger. "Knock-knock, Mr. Woodrow. Have you been pulling my zipper down?"

Nothing happens.

I nudge Elbie. "He can't manifest, remember?"

"Yeah, but if this is the guy, he knows how to make up for that." Elbie shakes the box. "Are you the dude I'm looking for? Come on, old man. Show me what you've got." He scowls down at the box as if expecting it to speak.

"Elbie?" Again, I nudge him. "Look at the shelf."

Like an invisible finger, something is cutting a line through the thick dust. First it makes a crooked line about two inches long. A shorter one grows out of the first, forming a Y. Then it scrawls an E and an S.

"It says yes," Elbie whispers.

"Let me save you some work," I tell Mr. Woodrow. "We're going to ask you some questions. If your answer is yes, then all you have to make is a Y. If it's no, then just make an N. Do you understand what I just told you?"

As the ghost finishes scrawling his Y, Elbie snatches up the box and holds it for me to see. "We were right. It was this guy right here." Gripping the box with both hands, he holds it up to his own face. "Hey, man. Why you keep pranking me? I don't know you."

Nothing.

"Answer me." He shakes the container.

"Calm down," I take away the box, a bit surprised at how heavy it is, and set it back on its shelf. "It's not like the man's going to write a whole paragraph in the dust. Just ask him yes or no questions."

"Yeah . . . you're right. All that effort wears ghosts out fast. It's probably even harder for the ones who've been cremated." He takes in a long breath and blows it out, then turns back to the shelf. "Did I do something to make you mad, Mr. Woodrow?"

This time the invisible finger draws a zig-zaggy N.

Elbie looks at me, his thick black eyebrows bashed together. "Well, that makes no sense at all. If I didn't do anything wrong, why is he harassing me all the time?"

"Elbie . . . you prank me all the time. Is it because I've upset you?"

"Well . . . no." He looks down at his feet. "I see your point."

"I've been thinking," I tell Elbie. "Mr. Woodrow was cremated, so he can't manifest. And like Mrs. Cowan, he probably can't talk either. What if all he wants is your attention?"

"Well, he's sure got that."

I look down at the shelf again. "Mr. Woodrow, is that all you want from Elbie? Attention?"

Another N.

"Well, then what?" Elbie says.

Since his question requires more than a yes or no answer, I say, "How about help?"

A crooked Y forms in the dust.

"See?" I tell Elbie. "Now, all we have to do is find out what."

Elbie slaps his forehead. "Arghh! Another needy ghost. There's all sorts of things this guy could want from me. And who knows if I can even do it?"

"Then ask him. If he can make letters, he might be able to spell out words too."

I turn back to the shelf and smile. While we've been talking, Mr. Woodrow has already scrawled four letters.

BERY

I look at Elbie. "Why would a ghost want berries? Are they even in season this time of year?"

"It could be a person. Do you want us to find someone named Bery?"

Another *N* appears.

"Maybe he means b-u-r-y, bury, like in the ground," Elbie says. "Am I right, Mr. Woodrow? You want us to bury your ashes?"

N.

"No?" I look at Elbie. "Then what *does* he want?"

This time, three letters appear in the dust. *ALL.*

"What is that supposed to mean?" Elbie mutters. "All what?"

As we stand there waiting for Mr. Woodrow to give us another clue, one of the boxes on a higher shelf wobbles, then falls over on its side.

Elbie shakes his head. "I don't get it."

Then another box goes over. And another.

I gasp. "I think he means he wants all of these ashes buried."

Y.

"Hmmm." Elbie looks thoughtful. "Okay, well, how about instead, we spread you guys' ashes all over someplace nice? There's a real pretty lake not far from here."

N.

"Was that no for the sprinkle idea, or no to the lake? Because there's lots of other choices. Folks scatter ashes in forests, rivers . . ."

A ghostly line scratches through the dust beneath the word *BERY.*

"I think he's saying he wants to be buried, not sprinkled." I kneel down. "Mr. Woodrow, if I'm right about you not wanting to be sprinkled, would you please make another Y for me?"

Y.

"Awwww, man!" Elbie moans.

"What? Your dad's a mortician. How hard can it be?"

"Not hard. Expensive. There's a lot of people on that shelf."

"Well, your dad helped us out with Mrs. Cowan. We should talk to him. Maybe he can help us with this problem too."

"Yeah." Elbie crouches down and gives Mr. Woodrow's box a friendly pat. "Hey, man, sorry I went off on you like that, but you were really getting on my nerves. Look, I promise to do whatever I can for you and your friends, but we can't find out anything until my dad gets back from his business trip. So, would you please do me a favor and leave me alone until I can talk to him?"

Again, Mr. Woodrow pushes the dust around.

HURY

"Hurry?" Still in his crouch, Elbie glances back at me. "What's this guy's rush? He's only been here a couple of weeks. Most of these other people have been sitting there for years with no complaints."

As if pushed by an invisible hand, Elbie's head suddenly tips backward, and he tumbles onto the floor. He scrambles to his feet and dusts himself off.

"Hey, man, I told you I'd do my best. Come on, Joey. Let's get out of here. I don't feel like playing ping pong anymore."

We head for the stairs, and just as Elbie reaches them he turns back, chin raised. "And by the way, your spelling is terrible." With that, he races up the stairs. Once we're back in the first-floor hallway, he slams the basement door behind us. "Telling me to hurry . . . who's that ghost think he is?"

"The name on the box is Marvin Woodrow, so I would guess he thinks he's Marvin—"

"Oh, forget that grouchy ghost." Elbie's hand swishes the air. "We've been so wrapped up with ol' Marvin-in-the-Box that we never figured out how we're going to sneak back into that library."

"Oh, we don't have to sneak inside."

"No?"

"No, I'm going to write Mrs. Cowan a letter."

CHAPTER 18

ON MONDAY, ELBIE and I decide Mrs. Cowan won't mind if we spend our recess time playing tetherball, so we wait until after school to take her our letter. As we stroll down the main hallway, we run into Miss Beverly mopping up a spill.

"Is Ms. Skyeblu back?" I ask her.

"She was," Miss Beverly says. She lifts the sopping wet mop head and lowers it into her bucket. "She tried to open the library this morning. Poor thing didn't even last an hour. That woman is fed up. One minute it was so cold she had to wear a parka, then ten minutes later she was sweatin' like it's August in Mississippi. And then there was the lights goin' off and on." She chuckles. "I messaged her on Facebook last night. Came back with some stuff about bad mojo and feelin' like she was being watched. I never felt nothin' like that in there, but I don't blame her if she refuses to come back. Today makes a week since it all started, and those maintenance goofs still ain't got no clue how to fix it. Did you know that the heater's blasting 24/7 now? Miss Juanita told me they've got a specialist comin' in from San Francisco tomorrow." She wrings out her mop and winks. "Oh, well. It's not my electric bill."

Elbie chuckles. I should say they'd have better luck bringing in an exorcist than more electricians. But I don't. Even after seeing our ghost videos on TV last year, most people didn't believe they were real. Dad said it was because faking them is too easy these days.

So instead of explaining that it's the ex-librarian's ghost who's responsible, something Elbie has warned me would only make us look crazy, we say goodbye and walk past the cafeteria toward the library.

As we stride down the long chicken-nugget-smelling hallway, I pull a thin spiral notebook out of my backpack. Elbie hands me a pencil.

"So how are you going to write this letter of yours?" he asks me.

I print Dear Mrs. Cowan at the top of the paper and show it to him.

"Well, duh, but then what?"

"I was thinking of something like: Elbie and I need to speak with you again. Please leave everything in the library alone so classes can start coming back in."

"Sounds good to me. Write all that down and sign it."

I do, but as we approach the library door, Mr. Minelli turns the corner. His huge football player head tips to the side as if he's studying us. "Hi, boys. Forget something?"

"Yeah, Joey left his sweatshirt on the playground again." Elbie smiles and pats my backpack. "But that's okay, we found it in the lost and found."

"Again? Didn't you lose your sweatshirt *last* week?"

I look at my shoes. "That's what Elbie says."

After a short lecture about being more responsible, he reminds us to study for the math test we're having tomorrow, then heads for the office so he can print the tests out.

"Okay, now, slide that thing under the door," Elbie says, once Mr. Minelli is far enough down the hall. "I'll keep a lookout."

I tear off the sheet of paper and push it through the narrow gap.

"Not all the way," Elbie warns. "If she doesn't see it, we need to be able to pull back. I really doubt if you want to explain what you wrote to Mr. Nguyen."

I nod and leave an inch of notepaper sticking out on our side of the door.

Nothing happens.

"Maybe she needs something to write with," Elbie whispers. "Stick the pencil under there too, but just halfway."

I do, and we stare at them for at least a minute. Nothing happens.

"Why didn't she take them?" I ask Elbie.

"I don't know. Maybe she decided to move on."

"But we haven't cleared her name yet."

"Really? I expected you to complain about not getting that bug book."

"Well, that too, but I've been doing a lot of thinking, and I've decided that proving Mrs. Cowan isn't a thief is more important than any bug book."

Elbie grins, all Tic Tacs. "Aw! My little boy is growing up. Don't worry, Jojo. She probably just doesn't know your message is down there." He raps on the door. After a few seconds, both paper and pencil quietly slide away. Elbie and I look at each other.

"Well, that was creepy," Elbie says.

He's right. But what happens next is even more creepy. As Elbie and I wait for the note to reappear, the door creaks open, as if pushed by a mild gust of wind.

"After you," Elbie says.

CHAPTER 19

OUR LITTLE VISIT with Mrs. Cowan doesn't take long. Afterward, we head over to Elbie's house to find out what his dad knows about our latest ghost problem, Mr. Woodrow. Elbie's mom tells us Mr. Bird is working down in the embalming room again. We walk downstairs to the main floor. Thankfully, the chapel is empty. We turn into the hallway, but instead of following Elbie to the end and walking down the stairs, I surprise him by stepping into Mr. Bird's office.

"I'll wait here," I tell him, dropping onto one of the chairs.

"What? Why? Come down with me," Elbie says from the doorway. "My dad won't mind."

"It's not him I'm worried about. If he's working on a body he's probably using embalming fluid. You might be used to the smell, but I'm not. What will your dad say if I puke all over his nice tile floor?" That's a real possibility, but it's actually seeing the body that bothers me most.

Elbie smiles. "I'll tell you what he would say. He'd say, 'Elbie, clean that mess up!'"

"That's right. So, if I stay here, I'll be saving you from all that."

"Oh, okay, since you put it that way. I'll be right back."

As it turns out, Mr. Bird was just finishing up, and it isn't long before I hear the basement door open and close. Moments later, Elbie follows his dad into the office. Mr. Bird doesn't have any services to deal with today, and he looks a little weird sitting behind his big desk dressed in silky looking gym shorts and a tee-shirt. Elbie takes the seat beside me.

"Sounds like somebody has a little problem with our boy here," Mr. Bird says.

I nod. "How much did Elbie tell you?"

"Only that he's been getting pranked by a ghost." He grins across his desk at Elbie. "To be honest, I'm relieved to hear it. With all that tripping and falling you've been doing, I was starting to get worried."

Elbie crosses his arms. "Yeah, well that ain't me. It's all Mr. Woodrow's fault. You remember him? He's in that last box of cremains that never got picked up."

Mr. Bird leans back in his chair and looks at the ceiling. "Woodrow . . . .Woodrow. That was a few weeks ago, right? Yeah, let me think." He snaps his fingers and points at Elbie. "Yeah, I remember now. His story's a lot like that Mrs. Cowan lady you asked me about. Old guy, like eighty-something. A factory worker, I think. Wife passed a long time ago. No kids. No relatives to speak of—at least none that cared a lick about what happened to his remains. Just the one brother who requested cremation, then never came in to pick them up. Turned out his wife didn't want them in her house. Told me he was really sorry, but couldn't afford to pay the price for a permanent spot in the cemetery."

I shake my head slowly. "That's what Mr. Woodrow wants Elbie to do."

"What? Get him buried?"

Elbie sits forward, hands gripping the edge of the desk. "Yeah, Dad, but not just him. He wants us to plant all the other ones too."

"Son, I told you not to use that word. People are not vegetables. We don't plant them." He clicks a few keys on his computer and frowns. "I could probably swing something for Mr. Woodrow, but there are twenty-one other boxes down there. Do you know what that would cost?"

"I know, Dad, but we have to find a way. Otherwise, that mean old box of cinders is going to keep after me. He's driving me nuts."

"I'm sure he is, but permanent interment for all those cremains will cost thousands of dollars. We can't afford that."

Elbie's eyes well up with tears. "So, that's it? I . . . I'm doomed?"

Mr. Bird reaches across his desk and takes Elbie's hand. "Oh, heck no. You're my boy. Just give me some time. I'll come up with something."

CHAPTER 20

WE FIND THERESA and Kerry watching TV in the living room. Tired and sweaty, I stretch out in Dad's new recliner beneath the recently installed ceiling fan and turn the speed on high. Elbie takes the armchair.

"Did your letter idea work?" Theresa asks. She turns the volume down on the TV.

"Yes and no," I answer. "Where's Dad?"

"He's at the pool supply store."

"Good," Elbie says. "We really don't want him hearing any of this."

Except for the ceiling fan and the recliner, everything in the living room is the same as when we moved in, including Grandma's huge throw pillow collection. As they usually do when watching TV together, the girls are lying on the sofa facing each other, their legs parallel. Two more pillows prop each of their heads.

"What did you mean by yes and no?" Kerry asks me.

"Yes, she took my note, but, no, she didn't write back."

"I wonder why," Kerry says.

"She unlocked the door and let us in," Elbie says.

"Blimey!" Kerry bumps Theresa's leg with hers. "Why didn't *we* think of that?"

"I know," Theresa says. "Too bad she was cremated. Even with that, her skills are amazing." She looks at me. "Sticking a note under the door was a great idea, little brother. How'd you come up with it?"

"Yesterday we met another ghost who's been cremated. He couldn't talk or show himself either, but he figured out how to write in the dust."

Kerry's eyes light up. "I'd love to film that. What did Mrs. Cowan write?"

"A lot," Elbie says. "And she's totally down with our plan. In fact, I think she's excited."

I open my backpack and pass over the notebook, which she flips open. "That's what she wrote when we asked her those questions you guys came up with. She made her own suggestions too."

The girls squeeze together and read what Mrs. Cowan wrote.

"I repeat," Kerry says. "Why didn't we think of this?"

"I know, right?" Grinning, Elbie leaps to his feet and drops his shorts.

At first, the girls' eyes go wide, but their shock fades as they realize he's also wearing a baggy orange bathing suit.

"Come on, Joey. I didn't put this thing on just to watch TV all afternoon. Let's hop in that pool."

CHAPTER 21

PRINCIPAL DAVID NGUYEN always stays late on Friday afternoons. It's a good time to work since, other than the janitor and a couple of diehard teachers, the building is empty. But unlike the teachers, who seem to have no life outside their classroom, Nguyen's work isn't school related. Friday afternoon is when he researches his bets for the Saturday races, something he can't do at home since his wife, Amy, would kill him if she knew he was gambling again.

Throughout the years, he's made good bets and bad, but the ones he makes tomorrow will be the most important ever. If the horses he picks don't win, those two thugs will do more than just punch him in the nose.

With everything he holds dear at stake, Nguyen's hands tremble as he loosens his tie, unbuttons his shirt collar, and clicks the Internet icon on his laptop. And there he stays the rest of the afternoon, glued to his seat, one knee jittering absently as he studies the bloodlines and track records of every horse in each of Saturday's races. Everything of value is noted with a fat round bullet on his favorite lime-green notepad. Two hours later, he has eight pages of notes.

After analyzing each scrap of information, he settles on three horses: Momma's Boy in the first race, Zippernose in the second, and Taco Tuesday in the fourth. He holds the pad up to admire his three selections. Satisfied they're all winners, he tears off the top sheet, tucks it into his pocket, and checks his watch.

Five-fifteen? The last time I checked it was four twenty-five. Not eager to raise suspicions with his wife, he shuts down his computer, then shoos the last teacher out of the building. Miss Beverly has already gone home since her shift ended at five. After giving each set of exterior doors a final check, he's ready to set the alarm remotely from outside. The hallway echoes with his footsteps as he walks toward the far end of the building, the exit where his car is parked and the security alarm keypad is located. But before he reaches the door, a banging sound draws his attention.

At the far end of the hallway, a door swings slowly closed, as if someone had thrown it open hard enough to make it bounce off the wall. From what he can tell, it's the library.

Who could be in there at this hour, and on a Friday? He'd said goodbye to Ms. Skyeblu more than three hours ago, saw her drive off in her yellow Volkswagen Beetle.

The lights are on too. Maybe the district electricians have decided to check things out. Stupid, since, with no help of theirs, the library has been up and running since Tuesday.

"Crazy maintenance guys," he grumbles. "Why can't they just leave well enough alone?"

Irritated by the men's bad timing and concerned they might mess something else up, Nguyen storms down the dim hallway, unappreciative of the new third grade art display tacked to both walls.

"Hello?" he calls out. "Albert? Jose?"

No one answers. Still wary, he marches the length of the library, past the check-out desk, past all five computer stations, and all the way to the fire exit on the far wall. Oddly, there's no evidence of disturbance. All the chairs are pushed in, the books are aligned like little soldiers, and every light panel on the ceiling is totally assembled with no sign of any ladders, tools, or dangling wires.

Obviously, Ms. Skyeblu forgot to lock up properly in her rush to get home for the weekend, and some freak gust from the AC caused the door to swing open. *That airhead and I need to have a long talk. It would serve her right if I ordered her back to school.* But there isn't time now. He's promised to take the wife out for a nice romantic dinner, and she expects him home by five forty-five. No, best to keep Amy in a good mood, especially since he'll be sneaking off to the racetrack tomorrow.

Satisfied that calling Ms. Skyeblu onto the carpet can wait, he decides he might as well check the thermostat while he's there and steps over to the wall mounted controller which assures him the AC is set for an acceptable seventy-eight degrees.

Okay, good, but that still doesn't excuse that frizzy-haired hippy from running out of here with the library wide open and lit up like a Christmas tree. Nguyen makes a mental note of everything he wants to tell Skyeblu Monday morning, but as he back strides toward the door, he stares, wide-eyed. Stacked on a table in the middle of the room are books. Hardbacks. Lots of them. But also picture books and paperbacks. All jumbled together, one on top of the other. Not exactly straight, but at least five feet of them. Sandwiched between the table and the ceiling, they form a bizarre tower.

Intrigued, he steps closer, wondering why he hadn't noticed it on the way in. *Is that her idea of art? Stupid. Even if those are old books for discard, it's coming down. It's obviously, an earthquake hazard.*

With no intention of dismantling the mess himself, he turns to leave. But before he can take two steps, the lights go out. *Do I have to call those maintenance morons in again?*

Surprised at how dark the place has suddenly become, he peers in the direction of the windows where thin slivers of light barely reveal the existence of the four rectangular openings. *No wonder those kids went nuts in here that day. Those new light-blocking curtains really work. Tables, shelves. They might as well be gone.* Realizing he's been holding his breath, Nguyen chuckles. *For a grown man,* he tells himself, *you sure aren't acting like one.*

Drawing in a deep breath, he locates the red EXIT sign above the library entrance and smiles, thankful he left the door ajar. The slit of light from the hallway is more than enough to guide him back if he doesn't panic. *And why should I? There's nothing in here but books.*

With slow shuffling steps, Nguyen makes his way toward the door, but, even with both hands reaching, he still manages to stumble into the computer station.

Careful, he warns himself. *The last thing you need is a black eye. After what happened at the track, Amy would never believe you got it stumbling around in a dark library.*

Reminded of his gambling mess, Nguyen sighs. *Who am I kidding? If those horses don't win tomorrow, I'll be lucky to come home with two black eyes . . . if I come home at all.*

Eager to be on his way, he reaches for the door, but the knob slips through his fingers, slamming shut.

"What the . . . ?" Again, he reaches out, but the doorknob refuses to turn. Astonished by its icy touch, he takes a step back and rubs his hand on his shirt.

This makes no sense. Even when it's locked, the door should still open from inside. Just another example of how inept these maintenance people really are. He turns and squints into the darkness. *Okay, where's that stupid fire exit?*

Grumbling to himself, Nguyen seems to bump into every table, chair, and bookcase as he rushes toward the back of the library. But that door also refuses to budge.

What's going on? He pounds both fists on the heavy wooden door. *I just opened this door two days ago. Albert and Jose can't be stupid enough to mess up both locks. And why would they? Skyeblu didn't turn in a work order. I'd have seen it, for crying out loud.*

As he considers his next move, a clicking sound over by the thermostat draws his attention.

"Is someone there?" He forces himself to stand perfectly still, but all he can hear is the wind whistling through the trees outside.

Humph. My imagination must be getting the best of me. Realizing he'll need Miss Beverly's help if he'll ever get out of the building, he pulls his cell from his pocket.

What the . . . ? How can the battery be dead? I barely used it today. He shoves the drained cell phone back into his coat pocket and with outstretched fingers, locates a nearby table where he pulls out a chair and drops into it. *Okay, think. The doors won't open. I can't use the phone. Maybe I could climb out through the air vents. They do it in the movies.* He stares up at the black void where he imagines the ceiling to be. *If I put one of these chairs on top of the table, I could climb up and . . . no. With the way my luck has been going, I'll crash through onto the floor, or worse, get stuck up there.*

Across the room, one of the acoustic ceiling light panels flickers, then springs to life, spotlighting Ms. Skyeblu's book stack from above.

Who did that? Escape plans forgotten, he leaps from his chair and makes his way over to get a closer look. *That's impossible. The whole ceiling is supposed to light up, not just one panel.* As Nguyen struggles to understand what he's seeing, the top book on the stack Frisbees off, landing at his feet. Startled, he gingerly picks up the book and reads the title under the one light.

Betrayed. "Is this supposed to mean something?" He peers around the stack into the dark and not so empty room. "Who's in here? Why are you doing this?"

Another book flies off the pile. This time it's *Stolen Treasure,* followed by *Thief* and *The Haunted Library.* These, he leaves on the floor.

Those titles. It's almost as if—no . . . that's crazy. He raises his chin to the room. "You aren't scaring me." As easily as slipping into his favorite running shoes, Nguyen shifts into principal mode, feet set wide and hands on hips. "You better be good at hiding," he calls out, "because when I find you, you'll wish you never started this game!" Moving faster than caution would allow, he lurches off into the darkness, both arms extended, but he barely gets five feet when something crashes into his head.

"Ow, geez!" Nguyen stumbles back, one hand pressed to the lump already rising on his temple. "That's assault!" he shouts out to the room. The projectile, a thick hardback novel, lies open at his feet. Squinting through the gloom, he notices something sticking out from between the book's pages. A photo. Hand shaking, he picks it up and holds it to the light.

Hey, that's me and . . . Sylvia Cowan? He recalls the day it was taken, eight years ago at the faculty's end of the year luncheon. Miss Juanita took it right after he presented Sylvia with the district's Librarian of the Year Award. *Why show this to me now?* He snatches up the book and gasps. The title is *Heartbroken*.

Sylvia . . . ? He swipes at the sweat glazing his forehead and smirks. "Good scam, but I'm not falling for it. Who's in here, and why are you doing this to me?"

No one answers.

"Oh, come on. This is so illegal. Unlock the doors and let me out of here immediately!" Realizing his words might provoke another flying hardback, he throws up his arms to protect his head.

Wait a second. That hippy's got a landline in her office. He dashes off to use the phone, but just as he slips behind the check-out counter, the office door slams shut in his face, rattling the window glass.

As if expecting a shock, he touches the knob with one finger before grabbing it. Like the fire exit's doorknob, it's icy cold, but more importantly, locked.

What is happening to me? Unsure what to do next, he slumps against the door, sweat-slicked forehead pressed to the glass. Soon, a humming sound draws his attention.

Nguyen turns slowly. The humming continues, as if a giant bee were hovering in the darkness ahead of him. His shoulders relax as he realizes what he's hearing. The new ninety-inch-wide motorized projector screen he'd recently had installed is rolling down from the ceiling. *Who turned that on? The controls are in the office behind me. Is that where they're hiding?* He turns and presses his face to the glass, but all he can see is darkness.

By the time the entire sixty-five inches of screen has descended, Nguyen's breath is coming in short bursts. Something above him clicks, and he spins around. From above the door, a shaft of light knifes through the darkness, exploding in a mass of color on the giant screen.

His throat tightens as he realizes what he's seeing. It's the video Miss Becky recorded the day he presented Sylvia Cowan with her fourth District Librarian of the Year award.

Stunned, he watches his younger self step behind a pedestal to praise the librarian for her many years of service, her dedication to Fern Creek Elementary, and the children. When he calls Sylvia forward, the system's new Bose speakers crackle with the intensity of so many claps and whistles.

"I couldn't have done it without your support," she tells the first-year principal as he hands her the plaque. "You've always been there for me." He responds by throwing his arms around her, and as they hug each other, a camera flashes. Probably the same one that took the photo he was just looking at.

After more applause, the recording ends, and the screen goes dark. With the heel of his hand, Nguyen wipes away a stray tear and waits, afraid to turn away, but even more frightened not to. As he wonders what to expect next, the projector makes some clicking sounds and the giant screen goes white. A moment later, six-inch black letters scroll up from the bottom, stopping at the center.

I THOUGHT YOU WERE MY FRIEND

Nguyen blinks hard, unsure what to think. Then, a second set of words crawl up the screen.

HOW WRONG I WAS

"Th-this is stupid," Nguyen sputters. "What friend? Whose friend?"

He looks around, but, except for the shaft of light beaming from the projector, all he sees is darkness. He imagines himself dodging around the bookcases to corner the prankster, but, instead, he stands there, a veritable deer in the headlights. *She's not doing this,* he tells himself. *She can't be.*

But the show isn't over. And if the meaning of the first two slides was vague, the third is perfectly clear.

IT WAS YOU, PRINCIPAL NGUYEN YOU STOLE THAT GRANT MONEY

"I . . . I don't know what you mean," Nguyen says. "Wha-what grant money?" The words burst from his throat, shrill and wobbly.

I DIED IN PRISON

Holding back a scream, the tendons in Nguyen's neck bulge as the lines scroll by faster.

I WAS INNOCENT INNOCENT INNOCENT INNOCENT

Even though there's no sound, the words echo in his mind. Then more words scroll onto the screen. With a groan, he presses both hands to his temples as if to keep his brain from exploding.

IT'S ALL YOUR FAULT!
YOU STOLE THE MONEY!
YOU FRAMED ME!
MY DEATH IS ON YOU!
IT'S ALL YOUR FAULT!
YOU KILLED ME!
YOU KILLED ME!
YOU KILLED ME!

Tears stream down Nguyen's face as he holds both arms out to his sides. "All right. I admit it. Is that what you want? Fine. I took the fifteen thousand and framed you for it."

CHAPTER 22

ELBIE AND I crouch behind the tall bookcase, mesmerized by the confession our wild-eyed principal all but spit from his lips. In front of us, is Kerry's new full-spectrum HD video camera. Wedged between *Charlotte's Web* and a dog-eared hardback I've never heard of, it's in the perfect location for recording Mr. Nguyen's confession. As if watching a particularly interesting TV show, I stare at the camera, frozen, as Mr. Nguyen glares up at the now dead projection screen, chest heaving, his normally slicked back hair sticking out in spikes. I've only seen crazy people in movies, but I'm pretty sure that's what we're looking at.

Kerry and Theresa are a few feet away. Two black lumps in the darkness, I can barely make out their faces by the soft glow of Kerry's camera screen. Theresa might be giving me a thumbs-up, but it's too dark to be sure.

We did it. We captured evidence that proves Mrs. Cowan didn't steal the grant money. But just as Elbie reaches up to turn off the camera, Mr. Nguyen starts stomping around, arms thrashing. From the look on his face, even *I* can tell he's furious.

"Okay!" he shouts. "I admit it! So what? You're just a ghost, Sylvia. It's not as if you can call the cops on me." His lips stretch into a Joker-like grin. "In fact, you can't prove anything. Nobody can. So, leave me alone already. Go off to library heaven or wherever people like you go! If you don't, I'll . . . I'll bring in an exorcist. Yeah, what do you think of that, you old bag?"

Mrs. Cowan must not like what she hears, because a moment later there's a loud crack, and Mr. Nguyen's head jerks to one side. With a gasp, he touches his fingers to his cheek.

"Geez, Louise," Elbie blurts. "She slapped him." He clamps his hand over his mouth, but it's too late. The words are gone and there's no way Mr. Nguyen didn't hear them.

"Who's back there?" The principal turns his head in our direction.

An escape plan. I knew we forgot something.

"Move," Theresa whispers. "Move now."

Luckily, both cameras are still on, and with their screens to guide us, the four of us cut our way through the black maze of shelved books, tiptoeing as best we can. But our advantage doesn't last long. Mr. Nguyen turns the lights on.

Not needing it anymore, I let the full-spectrum camera hang from the strap around my neck as we cluster beneath a large table in the back of the room. Elbie keeps an eye out for Mr. Nguyen as Theresa tries to call Dad again.

"What the . . . ?" Elbie whips his head around, still squinting from the sudden change in lighting. "Where'd that crazy dude go?"

I turn my head, but before I can answer his question, something big lands on the table, making everyone jump and Theresa drop her phone. We stare up at the table's gum-dotted underside.

"What was that?" an already breathless Kerry whispers.

Hoping I'm wrong, I hand Theresa her phone, but before she can get through, Mr. Nguyen's wild upside-down face lowers into the gap between two chairs, his black hair dangling.

"Elbie Bird! I should have known you'd be behind this."

As the four of us shriek, he lunges at Elbie, catching hold of his shirt. Luckily, the collar tears when Elbie pulls away and we scramble out the other side.

"Get back here!" Nguyen shouts. "Elbie! Joey! You . . . you can forget about recess for the rest of the school year."

We run through the maze of tall bookcases with Theresa keeping her phone pressed to her ear as she tries to call Dad. "He's not answering," she tells us. "But I left him a message."

"Call 911," Kerry says, already less wheezy having just sucked in a dose from her inhaler. "Here, let me do it."

She takes the phone from Theresa. Mr. Nguyen pops out in front of them. Everyone screams. With one hand, he grabs Kerry's wrist. With the other, he snatches away the phone and jams it into his shirt pocket.

"Students are forbidden to use cell phones!" he shouts. Still gripping Kerry's wrist, he tugs her around the shelf but stops suddenly. "Hey, you don't go to this school. Who are you?"

"None of your business." To my surprise and probably Mr. Nguyen's, Kerry pulls back her foot and gives him a hard kick to the shins.

"Owwww! Doggone it!" He lets go of Kerry to clutch his leg with both hands.

We dash for the main entrance, but the door is still locked, and with no other choice, run the other way—ut not before Elbie flips off the nearby light switches. Unlike us kids, who have cameras to guide us, it sounds like Mr. Nguyen is bumping into everything in his effort to get there first.

"We have to get out of this library," Theresa whispers as the four of us crouch behind about fifty stacked chairs. "If we don't, somebody's going to get hurt."

"Ya think?" Elbie says.

"She's right," I whisper. "I'm no psychiatrist, but I really do think Mr. Nguyen has lost his mind." Fighting back tears, I look up at the ceiling. "It's your turn, Mrs. Cowan. We did everything you asked. Please. Unlock the doors."

"Maybe she can't right now," Kerry says.

"That's probably it," Elbie says. "All that book throwing and slapping must have worn her out."

I signal for the others to follow and hunch off toward our left in an effort to reach the back door unseen. It would be nice if Mrs. Cowan has it unlocked by the time we get there. We shuffle toward the back of the library. But when we get to the door, Elbie still can't get it open.

"It's a fire exit," Theresa hisses. "You have to push."

In one quick motion, Kerry moves Elbie aside, grabs the knob, and slams her shoulder into the heavy door. It flies wide, and she stumbles out into the near dark parking lot. Theresa follows. Thinking Elbie isn't moving fast enough, I grab his right wrist and pull him with me. Too bad the principal grabs his left.

"Oh, no you don't," Mr. Nguyen growls, all red-faced and dripping with sweat. Like an angry dog, he bares his teeth as he tries to pull Elbie back into the library. But I won't let him. I hang on to Elbie's wrist with both hands, heels digging into the carpet as the full-spectrum camera swings wildly from my neck.

"Stop it!" Elbie screams. "Let me go!"

Kerry and Theresa must have run halfway across the parking lot before they realized we weren't behind them. Breathing hard, they soon crowd back into the open doorway.

Afraid for Elbie's life, I decide a threat is in order. "Let go of my friend, or the next kick you get won't be in the shins!"

Suddenly distracted by the unexpected odor of horses, I never get to do any kicking. In fact, Theresa and Kerry barely make their way back into the library when Elbie begins to change.

"What's happening?" I ask as the arm beneath my hands cools.

"I don't know!" Elbie shouts. "It started in my toes, and now my chest feels like it's charged with electricity. Am I freezing?"

As the horsey smell grows stronger, Elbie's shorts and Ninja Turtles tee-shirt changes, morphing into a purple and green jockey uniform. Beneath my hands, Elbie's bare skin is now covered with a silky-smooth shirtsleeve.

At the same moment, the icy current reaches my hands, and I pull them away with a jerk. Shocked in more ways than one, I look between Elbie and my suddenly sore palms.

Elbie's mouth flies open, and a familiar deep and gravelly voice spills out of it. "The kid told you to let him go!" As his lips form the words, I realize what's going on. Elbie's body is a giant sock puppet with Mr. Prendergast's ghost controlling it.

Limp-jawed, Mr. Nguyen gapes as more angry ghost words pour from Elbie's mouth.

"You're a disgrace to horseracing, you stinking pile of manure!" The ghost's rage powers through Elbie, and his right arm sparkles as the energy focuses there. Before I know it, Elbie's hand curls into a giant fist and—just like the hero on my Dino-Slayer game—pounds Mr. Nguyen right in the belly. A very impressive punch, especially since it's coming from a skinny little fifth grader.

A whoosh of air spills out of Mr. Nguyen. He folds over, grasping his middle, and as he drops to his hands and knees, Elbie's jockey clothes fade and he's back to wearing his Ninja Turtles tee-shirt.

"Run!" Elbie shouts, stumbling toward the exit. "Before he catches his breath!"

Now, I know how Mr. Prendergast managed such a powerful punch. He not only drew his energy from his surroundings, but from Elbie too. I catch him as his knees buckle, and with my arm around his waist, we stagger toward the door where Kerry and Theresa hop up and down, urging us to hurry.

CHAPTER 23

ONCE I HALF-DRAG Elbie over to Kerry and Theresa, they turn and run—straight into the arms of two uniformed police officers.

"Aaaahhhh!" The girls' screams are not exactly musical.

Looking almost as shocked as my friends, the officers rally quickly. "What's going on?" the stocky red-faced policeman asks. He looks at Elbie, slumped against me. "Do you need an ambulance, son?"

Elbie interrupts his panting to chuckle. "I'll be fine. I'm just a little tired."

The other officer, a much smaller blond lady with hair pulled back so tight it looks painful, peers into the open doorway. "We got a call. Something about kids being trapped inside the library." The brass nametag above her shirt pocket says J. Bass.

"Save us!" Theresa shouts. "He's trying to kill us."

As one, both officers loosen the strap on their guns, eyes on the open door.

"Who's trying to kill you?" Officer Bass asks, pushing us behind her.

"Mr. Nguyen!" we all shout.

Officer Bass directs us to stay put and takes a few steps toward the door.

"He's our principal," I say, still propping up Elbie, "but I think he's insane now."

With her eyes glued to the doorway, Officer Bass draws her gun and, just like in the movies, holds it in front of her with steady hands. "Fern Creek PD!" she calls out. "Principal Nguyen? Are you in there?"

From the darkness, a hoarse voice answers yes.

"Then please step out where we can see you . . . hands over your head."

The other officer takes out his gun too, and as he waits for Mr. Nguyen to come out, I try to read his nametag, but finding only one vowel in a herd of Ys and consonants, I soon give up.

After a few moments, a frazzled looking Mr. Nguyen staggers into view, one hand still clutching his stomach. "It's not me you should be pointing your guns at," he says, his normally smooth voice now croaky from screaming. "It's those kids . . . they broke into my library. And they attacked me."

The officers look at us kids and then each other before turning their attention back to Mr. Nguyen.

"All of them?" Officer One-Vowel asks.

Still a little bent over, Mr. Nguyen points a shaky finger at me and Theresa. "Not them, but the other two did." His finger swings in Elbie's direction. "See that kid there? That's Elbie Bird. He . . . he punched me in the stomach."

"Is that true?" Officer Bass asks me.

Knowing this is important, I make myself look her straight in the eye and say, "Elbie did not punch anyone."

"It's true!" Mr. Nguyen jabs her finger at Kerry. "And I don't know who the tall girl is, but she kicked me in the shins. And one of them threw a book at me. Hit me right here." He rakes back his wacked out hair, revealing a dark purplish lump.

Even though he's still a little wobbly, Elbie removes his arm from my neck and stands on his own. "*Nuh-uh.* No way. I did not throw that book at him."

Theresa steps forward. "Elbie wouldn't do any of that. But Mr. Nguyen did tear Elbie's shirt—and he grabbed his arm."

"Mine too," Kerry says. "I got loose quick, but I bet Elbie's arm has bruises. Show them, Elbie."

The policemen's gaze bounces between Elbie waggling his torn collar and his arm, which he's asked to hold up so Officer Bass can shine her flashlight on it. As Kerry suggested, a ring of red fingerprints stands out in the bright light.

Officer One-Vowel lets out a whistle.

"Mr. Nguyen . . . ?" Officer Bass's voice is soft but firm. "Did you do this?"

"Well, yes . . . but that was because . . ." His face pinches. "Listen, those kids broke into this school. They trashed this library. Look for yourselves if you don't believe me."

"Oh, we will," Officer One-Vowel says. He motions for everyone to go back inside.

What the officers see are a lot of crooked tables and chairs that have been pushed over, mostly from Mr. Nguyen stumbling through the dark. Also, there's the hundred or so books Mrs. Cowan piled up on the table, now scattered all over the carpet.

Officer Bass calls me to her. "What's your name again?"

Looking at my shoes, I say, "Joey Martinez," hoping she doesn't step any closer.

She does.

With one hand resting on my back, she says, "Joey, you look like a nice boy. Tell us the truth. Are you kids responsible for this mess?"

Wanting her to believe me, I do my best to ignore her touch and force my head up. "No," I say, holding her gaze. "And neither are the others."

"Liar!" Mr. Nguyen screeches, arms flailing. "They set me up! They . . ." As if a switch has flipped inside him, his arms drop to his side.

"What?" Officer One-Vowel tips his head. "What do you mean, they set you up?"

"Nothing," Mr. Nguyen mumbles. "I'm . . . I'm just upset is all."

"We did set him up," Elbie says. "To trick him into admitting he's a thief." He looks from me to Kerry. "Go on, show them the evidence."

As the officers watch our recordings, our principal crosses and recrosses his arms. He also eyes the wide-open fire exit.

"Wow," Officer One-Vowel says. "How'd you kids do all that?"

"Theresa and I made the PowerPoint presentation," Kerry says. "But Mrs. Cowan did the rest."

"Is that right?" He looks around. "So where is this Mrs. Cowan?"

"Around," Elbie says.

"She's a ghost," Kerry explains. "So, we're not really sure *where* she went."

"Mr. Prendergast helped too," Theresa tells them. "He's the one who punched Mr. Nguyen in the stomach."

"That's right," Elbie says, leaving out how the ghost used him as a weapon.

"Is Mr. Prendergast a ghost too?" Officer One-Vowel asks.

We all nod.

He looks hard at Kerry and Theresa. "I knew you girls looked familiar. Aren't you the kids who won the *Ghosters* contest last year?"

Officer Bass gives her partner a crooked smile. "Oh, I remember that. Always thought it was a scam."

"It wasn't a scam," Kerry says. "We really did—"

"Stop!" Officer Bass shouts, startling everyone as she chases after Mr. Nguyen, who's bolting for the open doorway. But before he can get there, Mr. Prendergast appears in front of it, arms crossed and smelling like a barn. Knowing Nr. Nguyen can't hear or see him, the ghost sticks out one foot and Mr. Nguyen stumbles over it, landing heavily. Before he can get up, the officers grab him by both arms.

Once they pull Mr. Nguyen to his feet, Officer One-Vowel looks back at us kids. "Did Mrs. Cowan do that?"

"No," Theresa says. "That was Mr. Prendergast. Turn on your camera, Kerry. He's still here."

Kerry does, and at the sight of the old jockey, Officer One-Vowel's already pink face turns the color of ripe watermelon. "Are . . . are you . . . ?"

Knowing they won't hear him, the ghost nods and tips his hat before turning to Elbie. "Sorry for putting you through that, kid. It was the only way I could think of stopping that fella."

"It was definitely freaky." Elbie rubs both arms. "But it didn't hurt any."

Mr. Prendergast gives Elbie a wink. "Glad to hear it, and thanks again for the great funeral. That trumpet fanfare was a real hit." He waves goodbye, and as we all watch, Mr. P dissolves into a mist and slips into a nearby heating vent.

Grinning, Officer One-Vowel thumps his partner on the back. "Do you believe in ghosts *now,* Janet?"

"After that, it's hard not to." She unclips a pair of handcuffs from her belt. "Principal Nguyen, you're under arrest." She slips the cuffs onto his wrists.

Everyone jumps at a loud banging on the fire exit door.

"Open up!" The voice is deep and familiar.

"This is the police," Officer Bass answers, just as loudly. "Who's out there?"

"Mike Martinez. I'm trying to find my kids."

The officers look at us.

"That's our dad," Theresa tells them. "He's probably the one who called the police."

Officer One-Vowel gets a good grip on Mr. Nguyen, then waves for his partner to open the door.

She does, and there stands Dad. His eyes go wide at the sight of our scraggly principal with his hands pinned behind his back. I think Dad's surprised. Maybe even shocked.

"What . . . what happened here?" Dad's gaze darts from face to face, then settles for ping ponging between me and Theresa. "I got your message. Are you guys okay?"

"Just fine," I tell him. "Sorry we worried you. Theresa tried to call, but . . ."

WITH MR. NGUYEN under arrest, I expect the police will let us all go home. But no. In fact, it's Mr. Nguyen who leaves the school first. Just not in his own car. Officer Bass radios for assistance. Seeing the second patrol car pull into the parking lot, Officer One-Vowel escorts our still struggling ex-principal over to the passenger door.

As we watch the two officers wrangle Mr. Nguyen into the car's back seat. Elbie pushes his shoulder up against mine.

"Check it out," he whispers. "That cop guy put his hand on Nguyen's head just like they do on TV."

"I think that's to keep him from bumping it as he's climbing into the car."

"*Humph.* The way that chump treated Mrs. Cowan, he deserves a few head bumps."

"Okay, kids," Officer Bass says once her partner comes back from handing off Mr. Nguyen. "Now, let's start from the beginning. What were you guys doing in here at this hour?"

"Yeah," Dad says. "I'd like to know that too."

We all step back into the library where Officer One-Vowel sits with us at one of the bigger tables. While the four of us are telling him our stories, Officer Bass is busy taking pictures of the mess. She also calls Elbie over to photograph the bruises on his arm.

Starting with Mrs. Cowan's first library rampage, we tell everything: how she held my bug book hostage so we would clear her name, the way I got myself sent to the office just to find evidence against Mr. Nguyen, even how we saw him get beat up in the racetrack parking lot.

Finally, the story ends, and Officer One-Vowel closes the e-tablet he's been tapping away on. "If it makes you feel any better, I believe you, but I sure don't look forward to sharing this back at the station."

"Then it's a good thing we have these recordings," Theresa tells them.

Kerry places her camera on the table in front of her. "Your boss can view them on my blog later tonight," she tells Officer Bass. "I'll post them as soon as I get home. Or perhaps you would rather I email them to you directly?"

Dad clears his throat. "Kerry, those videos are considered evidence now. Isn't that right, officers?"

Officer Bass nods. "I'm afraid Mr. Martinez is right. By law, we have to take possession of both of your recordings, cameras and all. That way, nobody can say you doctored them. You should get the cameras back within a few days, but until this is all cleared up, the recordings are evidence."

Kerry moans. "So how long will *that* take?"

Both officers shrug.

"Cheer up," Elbie says. "You'll post those videos eventually."

I reach across the table and pat Kerry's hand. "And don't forget, that's not the reason we did this. It was to prove Mrs. Cowan didn't steal that grant money."

Officer One-Vowel pushes back his chair. "Considering the fact that both recordings show Mr. Nguyen admitting as much, I think you've definitely done that, and once he's convicted, it will all become public record. Then, everyone will hear the truth."

Once the officers bag the cameras into evidence, we follow them out the door. The whole while, Kerry's arms are crossed. Coupled with the sour look on her face, it's safe to say she's not happy.

"We're through here for now," Officer Bass says. "Go home and get some rest. We have to stay here until someone from the school district office comes to reset the alarm."

Dad's car is parked a few steps from the library door. As Elbie climbs into the back seat, he turns to look at me over his shoulder. "Hey, Mrs. Cowan never gave you that bug book."

"Maybe she forgot."

Bang! Bang!

Everyone looks at the emergency exit door, which the officers have left slightly ajar. From the sound of the banging, it seemed that someone had knocked on it, but there's nobody there. At least not on the outside.

"Stay where you are," Officer Bass says. With guns drawn, they approach the door, and Officer One-Vowel pulls it open. For a while, they just stand there looking. Then Officer Bass bends to pick something up.

Even though the parking lot doesn't have the best lighting, I recognize what she's holding immediately. At least one of them. Elbie and I run over.

"I believe these are for you," Officer Bass says. She holds up *The Ultimate Bugopedia.*

"What's the other book?" Elbie asks.

She passes it over, and we can't help but smile. It's *The Thank You Book for Kids.*

CHAPTER 24

THE FOLLOWING MONDAY morning, Elbie and I run into a big crowd of kids near the office. Where there used to be six framed photographs of principals, now there are only five, and everyone is staring at the empty space on the wall. Mr. Nguyen's portrait is gone.

"Dang," Elbie mutters. "They sure took *that* down quick."

Everyone's talking about Mr. Nguyen's arrest. They know it had something to do with the stolen grant money and a past school librarian, who ended up taking the blame, but that's about it. "How did he get caught?" is the question of the day. Of course, Elbie and I could clear it all up, but we're not talking.

"If you want justice for Mrs. Cowan," Officer Bass explained on the night Mr. Nguyen was arrested, "then let it all come out at trial, and not before. That way, the lawyers will be able to put together an unbiased jury."

I Googled the word unbiased. It means showing no prejudice for or against something or someone. That's exactly what I want for Mr. Nguyen, and Elbie feels the same. So, as questions we can easily answer buzz past our ears, we say nothing and head toward our classroom. But keeping quiet is a lot tougher for Elbie than for me, and as we make our way down the hallway he squeezes his lips tight, as if the story will spill out otherwise.

A week later comes another surprise. As the class is doing its usual Monday march to the library, our normally straight line bunches up, and this time it's not what's missing that's got everybody staring. On the wall opposite the library door, Miss Beverly is hanging a newly-framed photograph.

One of the kids asks if the lady in the photo is going to be our new principal, but Miss Beverly shakes her head. "No, honey, this is a picture of—"

"Sylvia Cowan," Elbie blurts. Always one to enjoy an audience, he steps forward, grinning his big Tic Tac smile. "She's the lady who they first blamed for stealing the grant money. But she didn't do it. Mrs. Cowan was a very nice lady and great at her job. She even won the district librarian award seven times."

"That's right," Miss Beverly says. She pulls a hammer and nails from the small toolbox at her feet and flips open the cardboard box beside it, which, as it turns out, is filled with Mrs. Cowan's awards. "And here's what Elbie was talkin' about, seven plaques, polished and ready to hang next to her picture." She arches one eyebrow at Elbie. "But how do you know so much about Sylvia? She was already locked up by the time you got here."

Elbie must realize his slip because his smile drops away. "I . . . uh . . ."

"Oh, I see you're relocating Mrs. Cowan's awards." Mr. Minelli moves in beside us and reaches into the box. "Awesome. They *should* be out here. More people will see them."

Miss Beverly picks up one of the plaques. "I heard the school district is planning some sort of annual reading celebration for the old gal. On her birthday, I think."

"I heard that too," Mr. Minelli says. "It's the least they can do, considering how badly she was treated. Besides," he turns to look at the class, "reading celebrations are fun, right? Okay, everyone, let's go check out some books."

Saved, Elbie ducks into the library, leaving Miss Beverly's question unanswered, and thanks to Mr. Minelli, probably forgotten. I don't know who came up with the idea of doing all these nice things for Mrs. Cowan. All I know is that after everything that poor lady went through, she deserves the recognition. I hope she knows about it.

And it's not just the people at Fern Creek Elementary who are interested in our principal's unexpected arrest. The local newspaper had a big article on it, and even though Kerry is more anxious to spill our story than Elbie, she isn't talking either.

So, instead of a haunted library, the TV reports focus on Mr. Nguyen's gambling problem. Watching one of those shows is how I learned about pathological gambling. That's the medical disorder they say Mr. Nguyen has. As it turns out, gambling can become an addiction and can mess up your life just as bad as drugs or alcohol.

TWO WEEKS AFTER Mr. Nguyen is arrested, Elbie gets a mysterious text from his dad.

> Come straight home after school.
> Front door, not back.
> Bring Joey.

"Why do they want *me* there?" I ask him.

"I have no idea."

We ride over and find Elbie's parents standing behind the white picket fence that wraps around the funeral home's big front yard.

"Check it out," Mr. Bird says. "He points out the four large decorative rocks scattered around the yard. "We did it, son."

For what may be the first time in his life, Elbie is speechless.

"I like the new landscaping," I say, still not sure why Elbie's parents want me here to see it.

Mr. Bird holds the gate open for us as we walk our bikes into the yard. Elbie drops his on the path and runs to the closest rock. "These aren't just regular garden decorations," he tells me. "They're memorial cremation stones. How'd you work all this, Dad?"

"It wasn't easy. I had to get a permit from the city. And these rocks aren't cheap. Luckily, the stonemason owed me a favor."

Elbie moves to the largest rock and waves me over. I push the kickstand down on my bike and jog across the freshly-clipped grass. Like the smaller rocks decorating the front yard, this thigh-high rock is rough-cut and uneven, similar to any chunk of granite you'd find out in nature. The difference is the six round metal plates set into the surface. They dot the stone like shiny coaster-sized polka dots.

"They're bronze caps," Elbie tells me. "Each one has someone's cremains underneath it. See? They're engraved." He touches his finger to each of the circles as he reads the names aloud, "Frank Madden, Mary Louise Simpson, Wilma Pennington . . ."

Elbie turns to his parents. "So, everybody's here? Mr. Woodrow too?"

His dad blinks. "Who's Mr. Woodrow?"

"Daaaaad!"

"Come on." Smiling, his mom raises her arms and herds us around the side of the house toward the sweet scent of flowers. "We put your Mr. Woodrow over here, right between my favorite rose bushes. Sure hope he likes it. Unlike the others, he's only got two roommates."

Elbie jogs ahead and kneels beside the rock. This one has gray and white speckles too, but it's smaller than the others with only three bronze plates. I suppose that's what Mrs. Bird meant by Mr. Woodrow only having two roommates.

"You picked a good spot for him," I tell Mr. and Mrs. Bird. "The roses are pretty. They also smell good."

Elbie pats the bronze cap engraved with Mr. Woodrow's name. "Thanks isn't enough, Dad. This is perfect." He stands up. "I think Mr. W's at peace now. I haven't tripped over one thing today."

"I point down at his pants. "But your fly is open."

"Again? Oh, man!" Elbie's hands fly to his zipper. "What? No, it's not."

"Made you look."

Laughing, Mr. and Mrs. Bird each give me a high five.

Diana Corbitt is a retired elementary school teacher who has lived her entire life in northern California. She has two sons who, although grown up and out of the house, still live nearby. Ever since she was a kid she loved to be scared, either by movies or books. She started writing her first story in sixth grade. That one never got past six pages, but now that she's retired she can't stop writing. Her work has appeared in *Bewildering Stories* and *Encounters Magazine*. She had a podcast on Manor House and one of her short stories was published in an anthology entitled *Wax and Wane: A Gathering of Witch Tales*. When she's not trying to scare herself silly, Diana enjoys working with stained glass, travel, and going to the movies. They don't all have to be scary. Just not chick flicks.

CPSIA information can be obtained
at www.ICGtesting.com
Printed in the USA
BVHW03s1436211018
530811BV00001B/63/P